Jagger

By

Eve Vaughn

Eve Vaughn

Dedication

To my readers, thank you so much for supporting me, and keeping me going. I hope you'll enjoy reading this book as much as I've enjoyed writing it.

Jagger Grimaldi wanted Camryn Williams from the moment he laid eyes on her. He knows with absolute certainty that she is his bloodmate. The only problem? She doesn't seem to agree.

Camryn Williams hasn't believed in happy ever-afters since she was a child. Having witnessed the breakdown of her parent's marriage she shuns anything that remotely resembles a commitment. Too bad a certain vampire-warlock won't take the hint…although he is kind of cute.

A special family event brings these two together, but Jagger's need for Camryn has driven him to the point of madness. Can he convince her they belong together before it's too late?

Prologue

"You're not concentrating, nephew. If you want to perfect your skills, you'll need to concentrate. Pull that door off the vault, shatter it, and then return it to its original form," Steel instructed.

Jagger took a deep breath and focused on the vault in the center of the abandoned bank. He pushed his hands forward and pulled them back to guide the door per his uncle's instructions. It rattled and broke off its hinges, but it wouldn't budge any further. He growled in frustration. "I'll try again."

"Yes, we'll keep doing this until you get it right. This should be an easy task for you. As much as I loath to agree with my father, perhaps your mother did coddle you a bit too much. You should have more of a handle on your powers."

Angered by the criticism of his mother's parenting skills, Jagger found the fire he needed to rip the door off its hinges with a mighty heave of his hands. It flew off its hinges as if pulled by invisible cables. Using the anger boiling within the pit of his stomach, he liquefied the fortified metal. Then he combined each droplet and reshaped them until the vault door was back to its original form. With that task completed, Jagger returned it back to where it had been before.

"That was impressive, but as I said, your concentration was elsewhere. I shouldn't have to push your buttons in order to make you do a task so simple. You see?" And as if to demonstrate, Steele replicated Jagger's trick with the door with seemingly little effort and in far less time. "See? That is how it's done. I apologize for that jab because I know how extremely protective you are of my sister but there will be situations where you won't have time to draw on your emotion. You simply just do it. Do you understand?"

"Yes, Uncle. I'm sorry. I suppose I do have other things on my mind, but that is no excuse of course."

His Uncle Steele, who was a formidable warlock, respected not only for his old family name but also impressive skills, could be a hard task master and difficult to please at times but Jagger respected him almost as much as he did his own father. He didn't want to disappoint the Uncle who had been a surrogate father to him most of his life.

Steele closed the distance between them and slung his arm over Jagger's shoulder. "There is no need to apologize. You could never let me down. I only want you to live up to your potential. Your mother has told me of your adventures with the Underground these past months and she's boasted of how well you've managed to handle yourself. But she's also concerned for your safety. These Underground missions are dangerous. And if you continue to participate in them, you might not always meet an opponent you can best through talent alone even though you have an abundance of it. You must hone these skills so that you may get yourself out of any dangerous situation. It is how our family has managed to maintain our powers throughout the years. You are aware of the battles years ago between warlocks?"

"Yes, Mama told me of them. Grandfather's house was full of servants who had once been witches and warlocks, conquered by him and grandmother and drained of their powers."

"Yes. And because of that, our family always had to be on our guard. It's been at least a century since a Romanov has been challenged in a battle for power but we immortals live forever and some of us are known to carry grudges. It's why we must always be on guard. It is why you are now training with me. You have the added advantage of your vampire side, of course, but there are things you can do as a warlock that a vampire cannot. Do you understand, Jagger?"

"Yes, Uncle. I promise I'll do better."

Steel gave Jagger one of his rare smiles. "Good. I won't lecture you anymore today. We can resume your next lesson another time. Let us get out of here and perhaps we can talk about your distraction."

Jagger pressed his head against the cool glass of the large window overlooking the city in his uncle's Moscow condo. The chill against his skin was only a temporary relief for the sudden heat that coursed through his body. He wasn't sure what was happening to him but for a few weeks, he noticed strange changes within him. He was hit with heat flashes at any given time of the day, he grew irritable over the slightest things, and he found it more difficult to reign in his powers.

"Here. This may help you relax." Steele joined him by the window and offered Jagger a glass of clear liquid. "It's the good stuff."

Jagger took it gratefully and finished in one big gulp. "*Spaciba*, Uncle."

"*V chem delo*, Nikita. Tell me what's on your mind?"

Jagger made his best effort to smile but failed. "You haven't called me that since I was a child. It reminds me that you still see me as a boy."

"I apologize I made you feel that way. Of course, I know you're an adult but I suppose in my heart I'll always remember the little boy you once were. I think that is natural for all parents. You were always like a son to me."

"I know you meant nothing by it. I guess I'm being sensitive." Jagger returned his attention back to the view outside. And that was an issue. He'd recognized how testy he had been lately and there wasn't anything he could do about it and he didn't know why.

"Don't shut me out, Jagger. What's going on?"

"It's nothing, Uncle."

Steele clasped Jagger's shoulder and turned him around, forcing the younger man to face him. Eyes so light a blue that they were almost white, darkened. Steele firmed his lips into a thin line. "You're not a very good liar. Something is worrying you, is everything fine with your mother?"

"Of course. Mama is great. I've never seen her happier since she has reunited with my father."

"Perhaps, it's this Underground business your father and uncles have you involved in. When I heard you were involved in Dante Grimaldi's group, I can't say I was pleased. I'm surprised your mother and father allowed it."

Jagger shrugged. "As I've already pointed out and you agreed, I am no longer a child and am quite capable of making my own decisions. But trust me, they tried to talk me out of it. Papa even forbade me to join them but I refused to sit back and do nothing while my family is under attack. Besides, this *il Demonio* is a danger to the Grimaldi's and everyone connected to us regardless of whether I stay inactive or not, as has already been proven. I knew nothing about him when he basically kidnapped and brainwashed me into believing something that wasn't true. I was there when he and his minions murdered innocent people. And he would have killed me, too, had it not been for my Papa. It's why I'm back in Russia while there's a lull in enemy activity. I need to sharpen my skills because I'll need them when that bastard attacks again."

Steele was silent for a moment as if he were considering his nephew's words. "That's very admirable of you, Jagger. Believe it or not, you have the potential to be one of the most powerful warlocks in the world, coupled with your vampire heritage; you'd be hard pressed to find your equal."

Jagger raised a brow. "Are you saying I have the potential to become as powerful as you, Uncle Blade and Uncle Cutter?"

"Actually, more so."

Jagger snorted with disbelief. He'd yet to see warlocks that could match the skills of his uncles. He doubted he'd ever reach their level.

"I see you don't believe me, but it's true. Jagger, you were demonstrating a great level of skill at an early age. You were doing things from the crib that most warlocks and witches can't do until they're well into their teens. Had you began your training sooner, you'd realize that. My guess is, being that my sister bears the mark of Hecate, you might have inherited some of her skill."

His mother's powers had been suppressed by his grandfather for many years, but once they were unbound, they were like no others. "I'd never thought of it. Honestly, I'd never had to use my skills much other than to amuse myself because we'd lived mainly among humans but this…it's a lot to take in."

Steele gave his shoulder a comforting squeeze. "I know, but you will be able to handle it. Now, getting back to my original question, what's been bothering you?"

Jagger turned to face his uncle. "That's just the thing. I don't know what's irritating me."

Steele gave him a thoughtful glance. "May I?"

He nodded in acquiescence. Jagger wasn't thrilled about opening his mind to his uncle, but if one of them could figure out what was going on, then he could figure out how to resolve his issue.

His uncle lightly touched Jagger's temples. After what seemed like minutes but was probably only a few seconds, Steele stepped back.

"What, Uncle?"

"We may need to postpone your training for another time. As much as I'd like to help you, I don't think I can in this instance. My suggestion would be for you to go to Los Angeles and see your father."

"Why?"

"What's happening to you is definitely a vampire thing."

Chapter One

Jagger wiped away the sweat beaded on his forehead. Had the temperature gone up? Squirming in his chair, he tried to focus on what his father was saying. His lengthy flight from Russia to L.A. had been in relative comfort but since then his condition had rapidly deteriorated. Though he was happy to see his parents again after a few weeks apart, there was somewhere else he desperately wanted to be. Once he knew the root cause of this sudden change within him, he could think of nothing else. But Jagger realized he couldn't do anything about it until he learned about this malaise.

Niccolo Grimaldi must have noticed his son's discomfort because he turned amber eyes in Jagger's direction, clear concern within their depths. "Are you okay, son?"

"Is it me or is it unseasonably warm today? I understand it's mainly sunny in Southern California but this heat is excessive."

His father raised a dark brow. "You're hot?"

"Yes."

His parents exchanged a nonplussed look and Jagger immediately understood. It made no sense that he'd be so affected by extremes in the weather because his physiology made adjustments for that.

His mother walked over to him and cupped his faced in her palms. "Your skin is warm to the touch, *malchik moya*. But, I don't understand how this could be. Niccolo? What's happening to our boy?"

"Mama, I'm thirty years old. At what point will you stop referring to me as your little boy."

She dropped a kiss in the middle of his forehead. "Never. You will always be my baby forever."

"Sasha, you're embarrassing him." Niccolo lightly scolded his mate, although there was obvious affection for her in his voice. Whenever Jagger's parents, the two people he loved above all others in the world, spoke with one another, that particular emotion always lingered there. Sometimes Jagger felt like a third wheel when he was with them, but it was never because they made him feel unwanted or unloved. They simply had the kind of love that poets wrote about and singers described in songs.

"I can't help it. I'm worried about my baby. I haven't seen him like this since he was thirsting for his first blood."

His father's brow was furrowed, confusion etched on his face. "That was *la morte dolci*. He's already had first blood."

"Uh, Mama, Papa, I'm sitting right here. There's no need to discuss me as if I'm not in the room."

Sasha patted his cheek again. "I'm sorry, *moy malish*. How long have you been feeling this way? And do you have other symptoms?"

"Actually, that's kind of why I've cut my training off early with Uncle Steele. I was hoping to get some answers. He suggested I come see Papa because he would know more about it than he did. But now that you mention it, these symptoms are a lot like how I felt when I was in need of my first blood but worse. When I was in Russia it wasn't so bad, but it's gotten a little more intense since I've been back in the states. While I was training, I found it difficult to focus and every little thing seems to irritate me. It's been a constant battle to reign in my irritation with the most mundane things of late."

"But you've only been here for a day," Sasha pointed out. She looked to her mate. "What's happening to him?"

Niccolo slid out of his chair and closed the distance between them. Slinging a casual arm around his mate's shoulders, he kissed her on the ear. "*Tesoro*, would you mind if I had a word with Jagger alone?"

Sasha frowned. "Why? I'm his mother."

Now, Niccolo kissed the side of her neck. "I know, Sasha, but I need to have a man to man talk with our son. I promise to fill you in later…tonight." Their gazes locked and Jagger watched the meaningful look his father exchanged with his mother until understanding finally dawned on her face.

Sasha turned a bright shade of pink. "Ah. I see. Well, I guess I can find something to occupy my time. Perhaps, I'll go shopping and pick out clothing for GianMarco and

Maggie's baby. There's a cute little boutique in town that sells the most adorable little dresses with matching accessories."

"That sounds like an excellent idea, but I wouldn't buy so many girl outfits as you've been doing. The chances of Maggie giving birth to a daughter are quite slim. In fact, a female vampire hasn't been born in at least a century."

Sasha smiled knowingly. "But Maggie is certain the baby's a girl. A mother is instinctively aware of these things. I may not be a gambling woman, but I'd put my money on Maggie. In fact, I'll be taking your credit cards." She grinned at her mate angelically.

Niccolo rolled his eyes in mock agitation. "You're going to make us paupers with your spending."

"You're exaggerating. I could spend several thousand dollars an hour and not put a dent in your...our fortune. By the way, may I take the Ferrari?"

"Of course, *tesoro*, as long as you promise no more racing. My police connection is a tad bit overworked from having to erase all those tickets you've racked up lately."

She pouted. "What's the point of having such a powerful car if I can't drive fast?" Niccolo furrowed his brow and frowned. She quickly amended her words. "I'll be as careful as I can."

Jagger noticed she made no promises to his father. As he watched the interaction between them, Jagger was a bit jealous of the special bond they shared. Both had gone through so much to be together, but he didn't begrudge them their happiness. Sometimes, he wished he could have what they did.

He had gone most of his life without knowing who his father was, though he'd asked his mother about him on numerous occasions. After seeing how broken up his inquiries made her, he stopped asking but he'd always remained curious about the man who chose to stay away. He'd carried a lot of hurt, anger, and resentment. It wasn't until several months ago, when he experienced unexplainable changes within himself that he realized he needed to seek out the man he believed had abandoned him and his mother.

What he'd found himself embroiled in was an adventure beyond his wildest imaginings but, in the end, he had finally met his father and seen his parents reunited. Despite their short time together, Jagger had felt an instant connection to Niccolo and their bond was cemented from there, as strong as any between father and son. Though he loved and respected his uncles who had served as father figures, those relationships couldn't compare with what he had with the older vampire. In the few short months they'd gotten to know one another Jagger had learned to embrace the vampire heritage he'd spent most of his life trying to suppress. But *la morte dolci* was still something that he had yet to fully grasp.

Once Sasha had left the men alone, Niccolo took a seat on the sofa beside Jagger. "Son, when was the last time you got laid?" That was his father: straight to the point with little to no preamble. It was still something Jagger was getting used to.

Jagger shuddered as he remembered his last encounter with a woman. It was an encounter he wished to forget. "Maybe a month ago. I was visiting one of your clubs to check out the operation as you suggested and I was accosted by a pretty brunette. She was aggressive, going as far as to put her hands down my pants right on the dance floor. I'm a man, so of course I responded. She took me back to her place."

"And it's been that long since you last fucked?"

"I haven't had much time for anything else what with our missions for the Underground."

His father nodded. "Was the experience with your brunette satisfying?"

Heat flamed Jagger's cheeks but not from illness. It didn't matter that he and his father had grown close, it was still uncomfortable to discuss his conquests with the older vampire. Breaking eye contact, Jagger mumbled, "I'm not sure why you need to know all this."

Niccolo placed a hand on Jagger's shoulder and gave it a slight squeeze, compelling him to meet his amber gaze. "Humor me, son."

Jagger released a deep sigh. "It's almost too embarrassing to mention, but I could barely finish. She was a beautiful woman and I was aroused but performing the act was a chore. I-I could barely keep it up. It took more concentration than I've ever needed to be with a woman, especially one so beautiful. And yes, I was extremely frustrated afterwards. I felt like my body had been set on fire."

"This fire was it before or after you left this woman?"

"Afterwards?"

"Did you get hard when this heat engulfed you?"

"Yes. How did you know?"

Niccolo closed his eyes and pinched the bridge of his nose with his thumb and middle finger.

"What is it, Papa? What's wrong with me? I never thought I'd feel this way again after I received my first blood. But this is much worse than the first time."

"Who is she?"

"She?"

"The woman you're pining for. I imagine the reason you couldn't keep it up with your brunette was because she wasn't who you really wanted to be with. In fact, you were probably with this woman from the club to prove to yourself that you could be with other women. Am I right?"

Jagger's mouth fell open at his father's dead on description of everything that had run through his mind that night. "How did you know?"

"Besides a need for first blood, the most common cause of *la morte dolci* is unfulfilled desire. Your Uncle Marco experienced this with his mate. He was in a bad way; volatile temper, severe hot flashes, and arousal at inopportune times. The more he denied himself what he really wanted which was Maggie, the worse his symptoms grew. He became quite irritable and would often start arguments for no reason. By the time he finally gave in to his needs, he'd placed his mate in danger. Had Dante not intervened, Marco could have hurt her badly, possibly killed her. So it's important for me to know who this woman is, otherwise, you run the possibility of hurting her and yourself."

Jagger shook his head vehemently. "I'd rather die than hurt her. I don't think it's possible that I could."

One woman had remained on his mind since the moment he'd laid eyes on her. She haunted his dreams and even while he was awake he imaged seeing her everywhere. He'd memorized her every feature and often conjured up her smooth dusky skin, large soulful eyes, and inviting lips. Jagger fantasized about having her beneath him, with her dark hair fanned out against a white pillow as contrast.

His heart raced as he imagined tasting her plush lips. He pictured how they would look circling his cock. The mere thought of holding her in his arms gave him a hard-on of the likes he'd never experienced. Jagger didn't know why he wanted her so badly beyond the fact that he simply did. After all, she'd given him no indication his interest was returned. In fact, she'd been quite vocal in her rejection of him. No doubt she was lovely, but he'd been with women equally as gorgeous, yet she was the one who occupied his every waking thought.

"I'm sure you wouldn't—in your right mind. However, when one is in the throes of *la morte dolci*, you don't think clearly. You've seen your Uncle Marco with his mate. Do you think he would ever dream of hurting her?"

Having seen those two together, Jagger couldn't imagine it either. Besides his parents, he hadn't seen a more loving couple. "Of course not."

"And he didn't think he could either but from what I've been told of the incident, he nearly killed her. So I ask again, who is this woman?"

Jagger raked his fingers through his hair, positive his father wouldn't like the answer. "Well…"

"Son," his father prompted.

"Camryn."

Niccolo's eyes widened. "Camryn Williams? As in your uncle's stepdaughter?"

Jagger nodded. "Yes. I haven't been able to stop thinking about her. I knew from the moment I saw her that Camryn is my mate."

"Are you certain?"

"As you've already explained, I'd hardly be experiencing *la morte dolci* again if she weren't the one."

"I suppose not."

"You sound like you don't approve." Though his father's blessing would mean the world to him, Jagger wouldn't let it deter him if he didn't get it.

"It's just that…I haven't interacted with her much but I can tell she's not completely comfortable around our kind, Marco has said as much himself. She accepts Marco because he makes her mother happy but my guess is she'd prefer to keep her distance from the rest of us."

Jagger raked his fingers through his hair again. "I'm already aware of that, but it doesn't make me want her any less. I can't eat, sleep, or do anything properly because of her. During my training with Uncle Steele, I could barely wield my powers in ways I'd been doing since childhood. She's become my obsession. I even flew to Atlanta just to get a glimpse of her. I felt like a stalker, just watching her with jealously in my heart as she laughed with her friends and gave them the kinds of smiles I would kill for."

"Does she know you were there?"

"No, I used a cloaking spell so I would remain undetected."

"This at least explains where you went when you disappeared some weeks back. Am I to assume when you said you needed a few days to yourself that's where you were?"

Jagger nodded. "Pathetic, isn't it?"

"Not at all. Son, even though you've been raised as a warlock, you're also a vampire. We feel things more intensely than any other being so never be ashamed of your feelings. But I hope you know what you're in store for should you pursue Camryn. From my observance of her, she's smart, easy on the eyes, and has a pretty good head on her shoulders. But she's blunt and often says what's on her mind. I guess that comes from being young but she won't be an easy conquest."

"I'm not interested in conquering her. I want to spend the rest of eternity with her. Papa, in my heart, body, and soul, I know she's my woman."

Niccolo pulled away from Jagger, stood up, and paced the floor. His expression gave nothing away which worried Jagger. One thing he'd learned about his father was that he was a man who weighed his words carefully before speaking.

Judging from his silence, Jagger wasn't sure if he'd like what would be said next.

"Say something."

"If she is who you want—"

"She is."

Niccolo nodded. "Then you'll have an uphill battle claiming her. Camryn won't make this easy for you."

"I wouldn't expect her to. I can't help but hear the hesitancy in your voice when you speak of her."

His father stopped pacing the floor to meet Jagger's gaze. "Jagger, I may have regrettably missed a large chunk of your life but you are my son. You and your mother are the two most important people in my world which means I'll support you in anything you do. My only concern is that she's under Marco's protection and he'll allow no harm to come to her. This could potentially create a situation that could cause trouble within our family. You're in a precarious situation, *piccolo*, because *la morte dolci* is a tricky thing. If your need for her goes unfulfilled, it could mean trouble for you. Already, your body is going through changes because of your desire for her. You don't have much time to stake your claim before this illness becomes full blown."

"How much time do you think I have?"

"If you were a full-blood, based on the symptoms you've thus far displayed, I'd say two weeks, maybe three tops. But you're not. Your warlock blood might actually work to your advantage in this situation. It may slow down the process but I can't be sure because I'm not much of an expert on hybrids like yourself."

Jagger sighed, hanging his head in frustration. He wasn't sure if he could convince Camryn to take a chance on him in such a short period. He wanted to get to know her properly before even considering seducing her. Getting a woman into his bed had never been problematic for him in the past but Camryn was different. "I guess it seems my only option now will be to book another flight to Atlanta, but this time around, she'll know I'm there."

Niccolo nodded. "Just be careful and if you feel that you can't handle being around her without doing something irrational, get away as quickly as possible. Considering we'll be flying out to Virginia in a week or so for the birth of the baby, things will be extremely awkward between the two of you if things don't go as you'd like them to."

"I promise I'll careful, but I sense there's something else you're not telling me."

His father's eyes darted away, and Jagger knew there was something he wasn't being told. "What is it, Papa?"

"Unfortunately."

His pulse raced, and his breathing was now shallow. "What is it?"

"Just because you love her, it doesn't necessarily mean she'll love you back."

That was exactly what he feared.

Chapter Two

Camryn pulled out her cell phone to check the time. Terri was a half hour late. She'd warned her perpetually late friend she wouldn't wait more than twenty minutes for her. Besides, she had to work on her thesis and study for midterms. With an exasperated sigh, she gathered her purse and headed out the door. Just as she was walking out of the coffee shop, her girlfriend rushed toward her.

"I'm so sorry Cam. I had a sorority meeting that ran later than I expected it to. You're not leaving now are you?"

"You're twenty minutes late. I told you I couldn't wait around for you."

"I know but I swear it couldn't be helped this time. We have a new chapter president in my sorority and I swear the woman talks just to hear the sound of her voice. I was really looking forward to seeing you. Please?" Terri pouted.

Camryn rolled her eyes skyward. It was difficult to say no to one of the best friends she'd had since their freshman year of college. They had been roommates in the dorm when they were undergrads. They had ended up attending grad school together at the same university, as well, although they both had their own apartments. With their separate majors and different interest groups, they weren't able to spend as much time together as they once had, but they had a running date to meet at the coffee shop every week.

"I should say no. You know I have a lot on my plate at the moment but yeah, I've been looking forward to seeing you, too. Come on, girl." Camryn reclaimed the seat she'd just vacated once they were inside.

"Do you want to order something?"

Camryn glanced at the menu board on the wall. "I wouldn't mind just a regular coffee with whole milk."

"Okay, I'll go get it. My treat."

"Sounds good." When Terri left the table to give their order to the barista, Camryn pulled out her phone and checked her email. As she scrolled through the device, a tingling sensation shimmied through her body. With a shake of her head, she attempted to ignore it, but it wouldn't go away. It almost felt like she was being watched but she didn't bother to look around to verify. Making eye contact with strangers often lead to strange awkward encounters, at least in her case. If in fact someone was staring at her, she figured they would eventually get bored.

Terri returned with a huge smile on her face, two cups in hand. "Here you go, sweetie."

"Thank you. I really needed this." Camryn added two sugars from the bowl, stirred and tasted her drink. "Mmm, this is heaven. I'll probably be drinking a lot of this tonight."

"Pulling another late night?"

"Yep. I want to do well on my midterms. My Professor of Finance is on the board of one of the largest investment firms on the East Coast and he usually recommends the top three students in his class for internships in the company. I want one of them. I've heard that interning there will pretty much guarantee you a job in any financial institution in the country. "

Terri waved her hand dismissively. "You have that in the bag. You've got a head for numbers."

"I wish I had your confidence." She paused. This time the sensation of being watched was more intense and increasing with each passing second.

"I...whoa!" Terri's eyes widened.

"What?"

"Behind you. Hottie alert. It looks like he's approaching our table." Terri licked her lips and eyed whoever it was. Her friend was a major flirt.

Camryn was tempted to turn but didn't need to because she suddenly felt a presence directly behind her and the familiar scent of an exotic cologne tickled her nostrils. Her pulsed raced and her heart pounded. She'd only felt this way once before and she hadn't liked it one bit.

A heavy hand fell on her shoulder. "Camryn, we meet again. I told you we would."

The thick Russian accent left not a doubt in her mind who stood behind her. It took a considerable amount of her willpower not to flinch away from his scorching touch. As calmly as she could and without turning around she asked, "What are you doing here?"

"You knew I'd come for you. Won't you look at me so I can see your beautiful face?"

It suddenly occurred to her why she'd had the feeling of being watched. The thought of him watching her while she was unaware of his presence frightened and thrilled her at the same time. The latter emotion scared the crap out of her. "Apparently, you've already seen it. You were watching me, weren't you?"

"Is that a crime?"

"Stalking usually is." She couldn't figure out how he'd come in the coffee shop without her noticing. It was a sizable establishment but Jagger Grimaldi was the type of man one noticed right away. His commanding presence demanded attention. Jagger was the epitome of tall, dark, and sexy. He stood well over six feet, with a solid, broad-shouldered frame. His jet-black hair fell to his collar, caught between the edge of long and short. Everything about him was attractive, but Jagger's eyes were his most arresting feature: their amber gold was emphasized by the dark slashes of his eyebrows. Not that any of that mattered. She wasn't interested in any kind of relationship with anyone.

While she figured she'd eventually run into him again seeing as how his father and her mother's husband were brothers, she didn't expect to see him here. Not on her turf.

"You know this guy?" Terri's mouth fell open and then closed.

"Unfortunately," Camryn muttered still not daring to look at him. Jagger, however, took the choice from her, moving around the table until he stood directly in her line of vision.

"Don't you want to talk to him? If you don't, I'll take him." Terri greeted Jagger. "Hi, I'm Terri. Are you a friend of Camryn's?"

"You could say so, although I would like to be a lot more." The deep cultured voice sent shivers down Camryn's spine.

Damn.

"Please have a seat. You can sit next to me." Terri patted the empty chair next to her which Jagger took.

"Thank you." He nodded in Terri's direction but kept his amber gaze focused on Camryn.

With him seated across from her, it was nearly impossible to ignore him. Camryn hissed, "Why are you here? I thought I told you I wasn't interested in you, the polite thing to do would be to take no for an answer."

Terri's eyes widened as she gasped. "Camryn! That's no way to talk to your friend." She gave Jagger a brilliant smile. "She's not usually this way. And since I've introduced myself, what's your name?"

Jagger finally turned his attention to the other woman and offered her a smile revealing perfect white teeth. He captured Terri's hand in his and brought it to his lips. "I am Nikolai Jagger Romanov-Grimaldi, but please call me Jagger. It's my pleasure to make your acquaintance. As I strolled this campus, I noticed it's full of beautiful women and you, of course, are no exception."

Terri giggled. "Oh, you're charming. This guy is definitely a keeper. Like I said before, if you're not interested, I sure as hell am."

"Give me a break," Camryn muttered under her breath. She rolled her eyes annoyed with her friend's flirtation and how easily Jagger was able to charm her with a twist of his lips—his full kissable looking lips. As quickly as that thought popped into her head, she shook her head to rid herself of it. There was no way she could possibly be interested in this guy who laid it on so thick. He was free to charm whoever he wanted as long as he left her alone.

Terri glared at her before smiling at Jagger again. "So, how do you know Camryn?"

"Her mother is married to my uncle."

"Oh, so you're related. How interesting," Terri cooed, batting her eyes like a nitwit. Camryn wanted to throw up.

"I think the word fortuitous would more adequately describe the situation. Because my uncle had the good fortune to marry her mother, I met Camryn. I'm hoping she will allow me to get to know her better." Jagger said that last part as he glanced across the table at her, his gaze holding a wealth of meeting."

Terri seemed undeterred by Jagger's lack of interest in her and scooted closer to him. "I adore accents. Are you from Eastern Europe?"

"Yes, Russia."

Terri clapped her hands together. "Oh, I love Russia."

Jagger raised a brow. "You've been?"

"Yes. When I was in high school, my school choir went to Moscow to perform. I loved it. I even picked up a little Russian."

"Oh? *YA rad chto vam ponravilos.*"

Terri went from golden brown to bright red. "Uh, well, I'm not that advanced. What did you say?"

"Jagger smiled. "I said, 'I'm glad you enjoyed it.'"

Terri boldly placed her hand on top of Jagger's. "Maybe you can help me with my Russian. I've always wanted to be fluent."

Camryn had had enough. She wasn't sure why it bothered her so much to see Jagger and Terri banter, especially when she hadn't wanted him here in the first place. She gathered her belongings and stood. "Look, while you two practice Russian, I'm heading home to study. Enjoy your lessons Terri."

As if coming out of a trance, her friend turned her dazed expression in Camryn's direction. "Don't go Cam."

"I have to. You two enjoy each other's company." Without giving either of the table's occupants a chance to speak, she quickly exited the coffee shop. She loved her friend dearly but the girl was hopeless around men, especially ones as good looking as Jagger. She told herself that she didn't care that her friend had taken such an interest in Jagger. After all, she didn't want him, or any man for that matter, but still seeing them smile at each other irritated her to the highest degree. Maybe she was stressed over midterms. Yes, that had to be it.

She'd barely gotten a hundred feet from the coffee shop when someone grasped her shoulder. She didn't expect him to follow her or, even catch up to her so quickly. With an exasperated sigh, she whirled around. "What do you want? Shouldn't you be back there with your fan?"

Jagger offered her a lop-sided grin. "You almost sound jealous. Does this mean there is hope for me?"

"You wish. What the hell are you doing here anyway? Shouldn't you be somewhere else? Maybe annoying another person?"

He seemed unperturbed by her jab. "If I were anywhere else, I wouldn't be able to admire your beauty. You look even lovelier than I remember, Camryn."

"Oh, please. I'm not as easily impressed as Terri. What did you say to her to get away so fast? You didn't do any hocus pocus on her did you?"

"No. I just told her I had to follow you and perhaps we would talk another time."

"I bet she wasn't happy about that."

"Whether she was or not, is no concern of mine. I came to see you Camryn. I was polite to her because she is your friend. Can we perhaps go somewhere to talk in private? You said you were headed home. Perhaps your place?"

"Not a chance."

"Please, I need to speak with you. I've come all this way to see you and I know you don't owe me anything. But if you could grant me this one meeting, I'll say my peace and then if you don't like what I have to say and mean it, I'll leave you alone."

Camryn narrowed her eyes. "You're right about one thing. I don't owe you anything."

"Please, Camryn."

She really wanted to give him a piece of her mind for showing up uninvited but part of her was curious to hear what he had to say. "Fine, but you'd better not try anything. Marc will kick your ass."

He nodded. "I would rather cut off my hands than hurt you or make you feel uncomfortable around me."

"Well, it doesn't help that you showed up out of the blue."

"Again, I offer my apologies. I just had to see you."

"Can you save it until we get back to my place? Did you drive?"

"Yes, I hired a car from the airport."

"Okay. You can follow me there."

Chapter Three

Jagger hadn't meant to make his presence known to her in the café. He only wanted to be near her as it seemed the closer he was to her, his symptoms seemed to wane. He'd used a cloaking spell so that she wouldn't be able to detect him, but she'd been at her table in the coffee shop looking so incredibly adorable with her hair piled on top of her head in a poofy ponytail. Her skin reminded him of brown velvet, welcoming and begging to be touched. In his opinion, everything about her was perfection from the gentle curves of her body, her large soulful eyes, and her pouty lips.

When her friend joined her at the table, he tried his best to remain unseen but hearing the sound of her laugher killed his resolve. He could understand her wariness of his presence considering she had not expected to see him, but he was now determined to tell her how he felt. He wasn't sure how well she'd accept it but he had to try.

Camryn's apartment wasn't far from the coffee shop. The inside was small but clean and well kept. Framed pictures were strategically placed throughout the room. Jagger picked up a large picture of Camryn with her mother and a young man he assumed was her brother. "Good looking family. I look forward to meeting your brother."

Camryn crossed her arms over her chest. "You said you had to tell me something, so I'd rather you just did it and be on your way."

"I wanted to talk about us."

She narrowed her eyes. "I thought I'd made it clear there will never be any *us*. For my mother's sake, I have to be nice to her in-laws, but you're making it very difficult. I shouldn't have let you in here."

His winced at the vehemence in her denial. "It doesn't have to be difficult. Why don't you at least get to know me? My mother would tell you I'm a great guy." He grinned with his attempt at humor.

Camryn felt her lip twitch. She quickly turned her back to him. She refused to allow him to get under her skin. Nor would she let the scent of his cologne go to her head.

She clasped her arms around her body to get her reaction to him under control. She wasn't sure what was going on with her. It had to be a spell of some sort.

"Yeah, well, if she likes you so much, then maybe you should be spending time with her instead of me."

"My mother is aware of my feelings for you and she's very supportive of me being here."

"In that case, she's just as nuts as you are if you think that there's a possibility of us being together."

"How would you know for certain if you don't give me a chance? Look Camryn, I know this is sudden and that's understandable. When we met, I didn't expect to be so taken with you. But you've consumed my every thought since I've met you."

She shrugged. "Sounds personal."

"Camryn look at me."

She shook her head, refusing to face him. If she did, she wasn't sure if he would hypnotize her again with his intense amber stare.

Jagger, however, didn't seem to understand the word no. He gently grasped her shoulders and twisted Cameron around until they faced each other. She kept her head bowed so that no eye contact was made.

"What are you so afraid of?"

"You can ask that with us both knowing what you are?"

He sighed realizing he'd have to ease her in to the idea of being his mate, so he gave her the safe answer. "What I am is a man who wants to get to know you better. I'm a man who'd like you to give me a chance."

"What you are is something one would see in a horror movie. Your mother is a witch and your father is a friggin' vampire, and I have no clue what the hell you are!"

"I'm actually what's called a hybrid which means both my parents are immortals but not of the same classification."

"Whatever you are doesn't matter. My mother might be quite happy to be with a blood sucker but I'm not."

This was going to be much more difficult than he thought, but he got the nagging suspicion that it wasn't the fact that he was a vampire-warlock but something much deeper. The frustrating part was not knowing how to get past the wall she'd erected between the two of them.

Admittedly, he'd never had to work so hard for attention from the opposite sex so this was new territory for him.

Jagger grasped her chin between his fingers and tilted her head until their eyes met. Her mouth formed a perfect "o". He paused for a second to admire her beauty and barely kept himself from kissing her. There was an electric charge between them and he was almost certain she felt it too. "Camryn, what aren't you telling me? Why won't you give me a chance?"

She shook her head to loosen his grip and took a step back. "First off, it's creepy how you've been watching me and that you showed up out of the blue. Who does that except people who want to chop you up in little pieces and eat you for dinner?"

A smile curved his lips. "Eating you has crossed my mind."

"Eww, you're so gross."

He closed the gap between them until their bodies almost touched. "I think you'd quite enjoy it. Why else are you so wary of me? You were this way even when we first met. Why?"

She took another step back. "Look, I'm sure you're a nice guy but you're coming on way too strong. Besides, I'm not in the market for a boyfriend or any type of romantic attachment so please respect my wishes and leave me alone. We can be cordial at family gatherings but beyond that I want nothing else from you. And, if you can't respect those boundaries then we can't even be that."

Camryn maneuvered around him and headed for the door. She opened it and gestured to the outside. "Now that I've made myself quite clear, I think it's time for you to go."

"No." He couldn't leave just yet, not without fighting harder.

She narrowed her eyes. "Are you refusing to leave?"

"Hey Cam, is there a problem?" A young woman carrying grocery bags, whom Jagger assumed was a neighbor, stopped in front of the open door.

Camryn looked to Jagger and back to her neighbor. "Uh, no, my guest was just leaving. Right?"

"Actually, we were in the middle of the conversation," Jagger countered.

The neighbor seemed slightly uncomfortable over the contradiction and frowned with apparent concern. "I could call the police," she whispered low enough with the apparent intention of only Camryn hearing her. However, the woman obviously wasn't aware of Jagger's sharp hearing.

Annoyed by the interruption, Jagger muttered a distraction spell and directed it at Camryn's neighbor.

The other woman backed away from Camryn as if she'd been scalded. "Uh, I can see you have company. I really need to go put these groceries away. Let's catch up later."

Camryn's stared open-mouthed at the place her neighbor had vacated but then comprehension dawned on her face. She rounded on Jagger with narrowed eyes. "What the hell did you just do?"

Jagger shrugged. "A simple distraction spell. All she'll remember is walking straight from her car to her apartment."

Fire flared within the dark depths of Camryn's eyes as she slammed the door and marched over to him. She shoved her finger into his chest. "You can't just go around putting spells on people. What the hell is wrong with you? See? This is exactly why I would never consider being with you."

"What you're doing is using my powers as a convenient excuse to push me away."

"You said if I told you to leave you would. Were you lying?"

"No. What I said was 'if you tell me to leave and *mean it*, then I'll leave you alone'. And I don't think you do. Do you know how I know?"

"How?" she practically growled, not bothering to hide the hostility in her tone.

"Because you're trembling right now and I bet it's because you're wondering what it'd be like if I were to do this." Before she could respond, he pulled her within the circle of his arms and held her tightly against him.

"If you don't let me go right now, I'm going to scream."

He cocked an eyebrow. "I'd love to hear you scream." Jagger covered her lips with his. Camryn placed her hands against his chest and whether she attempted to push him away or not, barely registered. He was focused on tasting the sweetness of her mouth. Jagger gripped her ponytail and gave it a slight tug. "Open your mouth for me, Camryn. Let me taste you."

She remained stiff in his arms but he was undeterred. He slid his tongue along the crease of her lips and nipped gently at her tender flesh. With a sigh, Camryn finally parted her plush lips, granting him the access he most desired. Her taste was like nothing and everything he imagined all at once. She was sweet like honey, and spicy like cinnamon.

The hands that had laid flat against his chest were now tangled in his hair and Camryn returned his kiss, matching his enthusiasm. Their tongues circled and dueled with each other, sampling all they had to offer. The press of her soft breasts against his body was more than he could take.

Without breaking the contact of their mouths, Jagger gripped her bottom and lifted her off the floor, fitting her against his body so that his erection rested at the junction of her thighs. Without instruction, Camryn wrapped her legs around his waist, grinding against him. She was driving him crazy. He could smell her arousal and it increased his hunger to sample her pussy.

Not missing a beat he strode across her apartment and opened the first door he came to which turned out to be a bathroom. Camryn tore her mouth away from his and whispered breathlessly, "The door to your right."

Jagger captured her lips again as he carried her into the room and dropped her onto the center of the bed. He was on top of her in an instant, but this time around, he wanted to taste more than her mouth. He rained kisses over her face and along the side of her neck, enjoying the feel of her velvet soft skin beneath his lips.

"Jagger," she moaned. The sound of his name on Camryn's tongue was music to his ears. It made his already hard dick even more painfully so. She wiggled beneath him as if she couldn't get enough of his kisses and caresses.

Jagger slid his hand along the length of her, admiring the soft curves of her body. He pushed up her snug t-shirt to reveal two perfect, chocolate mounds encased in a lacey red bra. The sight was more than he could handle. "*Ty takaya krasivaya.* Your body is as beautiful as I imagined it would be."

She stared at him with lust clouded eyes. "You're not so bad yourself." Camryn ran her hand down his chest.

Jagger grasped her wrists and placed them by her side. "Grip the covers if you need to, but keep your hands here," he commanded softly.

"Why can't I touch you, too?"

He grinned. "If you continue to touch me like that, I may not be responsible for my next actions."

Once he was sure Camryn would follow his instructions, he reached into her bra and pulled out one plump globe from its cup and then the other. Her nipples were dark like black cherries and looked every bit as delectable. Lowering his head, Jagger took one pert tip into his mouth. As he sucked, licked, and nibbled, he rolled her other nipple between his thumb and forefinger.

When Camryn slid her fingers down his back, he pinched her nipple until she gasped out loud. "Hands, at your side, my beauty or you will make me lose myself."

"Feels so good," she groaned, lifting her pelvis up to meet his. The movement was nearly enough to make him lose his grip on the situation. He wanted to fuck her until all she could think about was him but he still maintained enough of his sanity to know he could only go so far with her. At least today.

He switched his attention to her other nipple, loving it with his mouth while he rolled the other one. Jagger couldn't get enough of her soft whimpers and moans. She sounded like a little kitten but he had no doubt she could be a tigress, if unleashed. Soon, sucking on her breasts wasn't enough for him either.

He wanted her pussy. He craved it.

Jagger positioned himself between her thighs and unbuttoned her jeans. Camryn stiffened. Sensing her unease, he locked his gaze with hers. "Camryn, trust that I won't do anything that you don't want. I need to know what you taste like here." He pressed the heel of his palm against her heated core. Even through the thick material of her jeans he could feel how hot she was between her thighs. "You're so hot between your legs. I bet you're wet." As he spoke, Jagger eased her jeans down her rounded hips.

With one big tug, he yanked them off and discarded them to the side. He then dipped his finger in Camryn's lacy red panties that matched her bra, sliding it against her slick entrance. "Yes. You're very wet. I believe I can help you with this problem." Gripping her panties in his hand, he ripped them off completely.

"Hey! This is my favorite bra and panty set," she protested half-heartedly.

"I will buy you a hundred more just like them. Besides, these are mine now. He placed the torn panties in his back pocket. Jagger turned his attention to her weeping core and licked his lips in anticipation. She smelled divine but he knew she'd taste even better. Jagger slipped off the bed and positioned himself on his knees. He pulled Camryn down the length of the bed until her cunt was in his face.

She was almost completely shaved except for a neat strip down the center of her vulva. Her plump pearl jutted past her damp folds, practically begging to be sucked. "Such a pretty pussy." He flicked her clit with his finger. "I think it's trying to say hello to me."

Camryn raised her hips in response, wordlessly commanding him to do what they both wanted most. Needing no further encouragement, Jagger gently parted her dewy folds and sucked her clit into his mouth. Her pussy was intoxicating. He nibbled on the little nubbin making her moan. Camryn threaded her fingers through his hair and gripped tightly, holding his head against her.

"Oh, God Jagger. What are you doing to me?" she cried out.

Jagger slipped his finger into her channel. She was so impossibly tight, he wondered how she'd feel around his dick, squeezing and gripping it until he emptied his seed deep inside of her. The very thought of being one with Camryn, drove him insane with need. Releasing her clit with a loud wet smack, he raised her hips and brought her legs over his shoulders. Jagger buried his face in her pussy, sliding his tongue deep inside of her sheath. As his tongue slid in and out of her, she gripped his hair even harder until he thought she'd yank it out. Jagger didn't mind, however. It turned him on that she enjoyed his tasting her as much as he enjoyed doing it.

He was relentless as he fucked her with his mouth. Camyrn trembled signaling she was near her orgasm but Jagger was far from finished with her. He swiped her pussy from her clit to the puckered bud of her anus. He wanted to know every inch of her. He pressed his tongue against the tight ring of her ass circling it and reveling in the tangy flavor of her.

"Jagger, I can't take it. I'm going to…oh. My. God!"

Jagger squeezed her clit with his fingers as he continued to lick her pussy and ass. She started to shake. She screamed as she climaxed. Jagger lapped up every drop of her essence. It was like the sweetest ambrosia. He was rewarded with a second orgasm from Camryn as her body shook and she cried out his name. Only after she released the death grip on his hair did he slow down. If he went any further, he would end up fucking her and he had to get out of here while he still had some control.

Reluctantly, he pulled away from her. Jagger stood and pulled Camryn to her feet and held her against him in a tight embrace. "I don't want to leave you but I have to go now. I want to make love to you, but now is not the right time. Just know when you allowed me into your home, I hadn't intended for things to go so far."

Camryn was silent for a moment, but suddenly, she pushed him away. Because he wasn't expecting her to, Jagger stumbled backward, nearly losing his footing. "What did you do to me?" Gone was the mewling kitten that had enjoyed the pleasure he'd provided. In its place was a Fury.

"I sampled your delectable pussy. Did I not say you'd enjoy it?"

She glared at him. "You know what I mean. What did you do to me? You must have cast some kind of spell on me to make me respond to you the way I did."

For a second Jagger thought she might be joking, but the expression on her face was quite serious. It was apparent she had gone back to her state of denial. "I didn't do anything besides make you feel good. Very good. In fact, it was you who was gripping me so tight to that beautiful cunt that I couldn't pull away even if I wanted to, at least not without losing a chunk of hair."

"You're lying."

"The only person who's lying here is you, to yourself. Believe it or not I would never use my powers to persuade you to do something you didn't want to do. And truth be told, I couldn't if I wanted to. I still have quite a bit of training to do before I'm at a skill level to pull off the power of manipulation or I have to live at least a couple hundred more years before I can glamour people."

"Bullshit. What was that thing you did to my neighbor?"

"As I already told you, it was a mere distraction spell. It temporarily makes one forget. I can't make someone do something they don't want to. Your neighbor was easily susceptible to that particular spell because she really didn't want to get involved in the first place. She was simply asking if you needed help to be polite."

"And how the hell would you know?"

"I'm good at reading people. Like now, for instance, you're so certain I have tricked my way into your bed, when you should be asking yourself why you're fighting this attraction so hard. You enjoyed what happened as much as I did and hopefully, you will eventually accept it. There's so much I wanted to tell you, but I see you're not ready for it."

"Whatever it is you have to say, I don't want to hear it. I want you to go and this time, I mean it." She folded her arms over her chest, covering her breasts.

The wall she'd erected was firmly back in place and there was no getting past it while she was still in deep denial. It was disappointing that he couldn't share what was going on with her, but this trip wasn't a total bust. He discovered that she wasn't as immune to him as she'd let on earlier.

"Fine. I'll leave but whether you'd like it to be or not, this isn't over." Jagger strode out the room not looking back, in fear that the sight of her would make him lose control. As he left her apartment, with her panties still in his back pocket, he licked his lips, savoring the taste of her.

No. This was far from over.

Chapter Four

"Don't I get a say in this?" Christine asked her mate as he paced the length of their bedroom floor. It still took some getting used to, calling it their bedroom when only a few short months ago her life was nearly cut short by an inoperable brain tumor. Now, she not only had a clean bill of health, but she was a vampire. Along with her newly attained immortality, she had a family, a new home, and the man of her dreams, who unfortunately was being a huge butthead at the moment.

Romeo shook his head. "No. Not in this instance. I want you to cease all contact with that woman. She's dangerous and I don't want her anywhere near you or our children."

Ever since the adoption of their children became official, Romeo had suddenly become extremely overprotective. She knew he was just trying to do his best to protect them but he was being a bit boorish about it. "You're not being fair, Romeo. I've known Nya long before I met you and she's never harmed me. If it weren't for her, you wouldn't have known about my condition. I owe my life to her and for that you should at least tolerate her."

"She's on the wrong side of this battle. Listen to me, Christine I'm not trying to dictate who you should and shouldn't be friends with but—"

"No buts. That's exactly what you're doing. You're telling me I can't be friends with someone who hasn't been anything but good to me."

"And you trust her around our children? Because I sure as hell don't."

"I know she wouldn't harm them. She hasn't yet." Christine turned her back to hide her expression. She'd said too much.

"Christine... what aren't you telling me?"

"Nothing."

"Look at me."

She slowly turned back to face him, hoping her expression was neutral.

"She's been around the children, hasn't she?"

"Yes! I didn't think it was such a big deal. When you left for a couple days on Underground business a couple weeks ago, she showed up."

Romeo grasped Christine by the shoulders. His dark blue eyes were nearly black in his anger. "How could you let that woman around my kids? Are you insane?"

Christine, however, refused to be intimidated. "They're my children, too, and I, also, have the right to dictate who can and can't have access to them. When I was at my lowest, she was there for me. She was my shoulder to cry on and my confidant. That hasn't changed just because you think she's evil. She isn't. She's my best friend. What's changed between now and the last time you saw her? You two were almost cordial with one another."

Romeo raked his fingers through his short blond locks. "Christine, I appreciate that she means something to you. I will forever be in her debt that she notified me of your condition. But as grateful as I am, it doesn't erase the fact that she's in league with a very powerful rogue, the same rogue who has tried to destroy our family for centuries."

Christine was able to read between the lines and figured there was more to what he was not saying than what was actually being verbalized. "Why do I get the impression it's you who are hiding something from me? Was it the trip? You found out something then, didn't you?"

He released a heavy sigh and took a seat in the nearest chair. Christine walked over to him and placed her hands on his shoulders. "What did you find out?"

"I wanted to keep this from you because I know how much she means to you, but do you remember when I told you about the big confrontation in Scotland?"

She nodded slowly. "Yes, *il Demonio* escaped."

"With the help of *il Diavolo*, and standing with him was your friend, Nya. It made no sense to me that she'd be helping our enemy if she, too, wasn't connected to him. I only called a temporary truce with her for your sake because of your illness. But as the two of us got settled and the adoption had gone through, it nagged me that she might pop up again as you say she does. I found it to be a hell of a coincidence that she would befriend you, you who happened to be my mate."

"Hold up. You're not suggesting she's been using me to get to you because I knew her way before I knew you."

"Yes, I know. And as it turns out, it was just a coincidence. Still, the time I was away wasn't so much an Underground mission as a fact gathering trip. I needed to find out more about this mysterious femme."

Christine was almost too frightened to ask but she did anyway. "Yes, and what did you find out exactly?"

"*Il Demonio*, the architect of just about every tragedy that befell the Grimaldi family also goes by the name Adonis. I got some info that suggested that he has a mate—by the name of Nya."

Christine shook her head in disbelief. "That can't be true. She would have mentioned him, said something to me at least."

Romeo nodded. "Kind of makes you wonder what else she's hiding. So you can understand why I don't want this woman around you or the children, again. It might have been a coincidence of how you met and she very well may have been your friend but I can't be certain she's not getting secrets to take back to her lover."

The thought of being used by someone she held in high regard hurt more than Christine could put into words but her heart told her that Romeo was wrong. She wrapped her arms around her husband's shoulders and rested her head on top of his. "Romeo, you know I love you with everything in my being. I would literally cease to exist without you. You and the children are my life and I'm glad you want to protect us, but my gut is telling me there's more to this than what some informant told you."

Romeo shrugged her off and pulled her onto his lap. He gripped her face and pressed his lips against hers. Heat blazed through her body from the simple contact. Romeo excited her in ways no man ever could. She whimpered when he pulled away and gave her a thoughtful look. He casually brushed a lock of hair from her forehead. "One of the things I love about you is the way you want to see good in other people but I think you're backing the wrong person in this fight."

"Before you write her off, would you at least hear me out?"

He didn't seem inclined to listen to her point of view but finally, with a sigh, he nodded. "Fine."

"You don't know her like I do. It's true that Nya doesn't share a lot about herself with me but I have been able to glean from little pieces here and there that her situation isn't a happy one. If she's with Adonis and you've been told she is, I'm sure it isn't by choice."

"If that's possible, how is she able to come and go as she pleases?"

"I think he keeps watch over her."

"All the more reason you shouldn't be around her. If Adonis has his minions following her, it stands to reason he would indirectly have a way to get to you as well."

"For the length of time I've known her, I've never seen her show much emotion, but I swear she had tears in her eyes when she saw the kids. She's always had a bit of a sad look in her eyes but I swear I'd never seen her like that. In fact, she told me how beautiful they were and that she had to leave. No other explanation. Something's happened to her. Maybe he's abusive."

"Nya strikes me as the type of woman who can take care of herself. Look, Christine, your heart is in the right place but you can't save everyone. My duty as your mate is to protect you and our children and that's what I have to do."

Christine lowered her head, disappointed she hadn't changed his stance. Romeo caught her chin between his fingers and raised it until their eyes met. "Baby, I know how much she means to you. If after the dust settles and we get Adonis out of the way and she's all you say she is, then we'll revisit this conversation. Okay?"

"But—"

He placed a finger over her lips. "I can think of something more pleasurable we could be doing besides talking." Romeo slipped his hand beneath her blouse and fondled her breasts.

Christine giggled. "You have a one track mind." She moaned when he nuzzled her neck and eased his fingers inside her bra. Her core throbbed with need. She could probably live for a million years and never get tired of his touch.

"What are you guys doing?" Jaxson stood in the middle of the room shooting them an accusatory stare.

Even with her newly acquired, super-sensitive vampire hearing, she still hadn't noticed her six-year-old enter the living room. Immediately, she yanked Romeo's hand from under her shirt. Her cheeks burned with embarrassment.

Romeo, however, seemed unaffected. He grinned at the little boy. "What can we do for you son? Shouldn't you be sleeping? It's well past your bedtime."

"I wanted some water. What were you guys doing?"

"Mommy and I were about to make l—"

"Cookies!" Christine interrupted, still mortified at being caught. She shoved her elbow into Romeo's ribcage.

"I've never seen anyone make cookies like that before. I think you two were about to do it." Jaxson grinned, revealing two missing teeth.

Christine glared at her husband who shrugged before turning back to her son. "Where did you hear that term?"

"At school. Brandon Jones showed us a video on his cell phone during recess. He said the people were doing it."

He seemed quite proud of himself to know that. "Can I have a phone, too?"

"Absolutely not. There's no reason a six year old should have a phone. And first thing in the morning, I'm going to your school and having a long talk with your principal about what's happening at recess. Now, let's go get you that water." Christine slid off Romeo's lap. Romeo, of course, was no help. He looked to be on the verge of laughter. Her son was precocious and would probably be more than a handful as he grew up. But she wouldn't change her family for the world.

"If you ask me, I think it's disgusting that your mother is having a baby at her age. She's not exactly fit either. Imagine how much weight she's probably packed on. That can't be healthy." Eugene Williams followed his scathing statement by downing his fourth glass of wine.

Camryn pulled her phone from the side of her purse and gave it a glance to check the time. Even though she'd only been here at the restaurant with her father for just under an hour, it felt like she'd been here a lot longer. She thought her father would be over his bitterness by now but it seemed he wasn't ready to let things be. Ever since he'd learned his ex-wife was happy in her new marriage and having a baby, all he ever did was speak of her in a derogatory way. It had gotten so uncomfortable for Camryn, that she rarely called him anymore. The only reason she'd accepted his dinner invitation was to be polite. She was after all in town for the next couple weeks, for the impending birth of her new sibling.

"Daddy, she's not the old lady you're implying she is. Mom just turned forty-one and she's in perfect health. In fact, I've never seen her look better. Besides, lots of women are having their first child well beyond that." Camryn omitted the part where her mother was now a vampire who could probably have children for centuries to come, but that was another issue altogether.

"Well, she still ought to be ashamed of herself. I'm surprised things have lasted this long between her and that gigolo. I don't trust that guy. He's way too slick. And what the heck is it that he sees in your mother? It's not like she has money or anything."

Camryn was fast losing patience with all the barbs directed at her mother. "That 'gigolo' is her husband, and I doubt Marc is going to let her out of his grasp anytime soon. They love each other very much. And as far as money goes, he's got plenty to support them."

Eugene released a loud belch, drawing stares from the other diners closest to their table. Camryn recoiled in disgust. Her father was once someone who prided himself on his appearance and, normally appeared refined. He'd worn tailor-made suits and expensive Italian leather shoes. But, the man before her was unkempt and seemed to be a shadow of the man she once knew. His bloodshot eyes were ringed with red and it didn't appear as if he'd had a proper hair cut in a couple of months. His shirt was stained and his jacket was wrinkled.

Camryn wished she'd driven straight to her mother's house instead of agreeing to this dinner. She loved her father, but there were times like this when she didn't like him very much. It didn't help matters that she still hadn't come to terms with all the years he'd treated her mother like dirt with his verbal abuse, cheating, and neglect. It had caused Camryn to resent her mother just as much for putting up with it.

Fortunately, with some insight and soul searching, Camryn had at last come to an understanding with her mother, and now they were closer than ever. Her sense of fair play, unfortunately, made it impossible for her to ignore her father even if he didn't always make sound decisions. He'd left her mom for a younger woman, whom he'd then divorced within a month, stating that he'd never meant to marry her in the first place. He had told Camryn that his second ex-wife had coerced him even though he'd been quite willing to walk out on his family. Currently, he was dating a woman only a year older than Camryn's twenty-two. Camryn had only met the woman once and she didn't seem like a woman in love. If Camryn were a betting person, she'd put money on that relationship not lasting the remainder of the year.

Her father slouched in his chair. "You mark my words, young lady, when that creature she calls herself married to gets rid of her—and he will—I'm not taking her back." His voice was as belligerent as his words.

Camryn knew that last part was a lie. She knew her father well. He'd expected Maggie to wait around for him to come back to her and be miserable while waiting so he could snap his fingers and graciously offer a reconciliation. He wasn't fooling anyone. "Um, Daddy, Mom doesn't want you back, and like I said, she and Marc are very happy together. They can't keep their hands off of each other. Even though, it still freaks me out to see my mother making out all over the place with her man, they're actually very cute together. And, Mom smiles all the time. I've never seen her happier. The baby is going to come any day now and that will only cement the tight bond they already have. Face it, Daddy, Mom has moved on and even if something were to happen to that relationship which I seriously doubt, she wouldn't want you back either."

She sighed. "Do you think we can change the subject now? You've been talking about Mom since we got here. Have you forgotten you were the one who walked away? Could it be that you didn't think she'd move on with her life and find happiness?"

"She knew I'd come back to her eventually," he said sulkily, reminding Camryn of a two year old instead of the middle-aged man he was.

"Did she? You told her you were engaged and then you served her with divorce papers. What was she supposed to think? Had I been her, I would have gotten rid of you a long time ago. You weren't the best husband and neither of you were happy. Why can't you just be happy for her?"

"Why should I be? It sure didn't take her long to hook up with that man she's with. I bet she was cheating all along while playing the victim."

"You're projecting. The only one who had been unfaithful in the marriage was you."

He shrugged seeming unrepentant. "It's not like any red-blooded man could blame me. She'd let herself go. What did she expect me to do? Hopefully, that baby she had doesn't take after her."

That was it! Camryn had had enough of her father's drunken comments. "Look, I didn't really want to be here in the first place but I figured since you're my Dad, maybe we could have a nice dinner together but all you've done is talk about Mom. Your obsession with her is kind of sad. It's your fault for not realizing the treasure you had when you were together, so you have no room to complain. I need to leave. Do yourself a favor and call a cab home."

His eyes narrowed to angry slits. "Don't tell me what to do, young lady. Have you forgotten who writes the checks to your grad school?"

"Have *you* forgotten I only have two semesters left? And you've already sent a check for the next one, which has already cleared. I can easily work more hours at the student union to pay for the last one myself."

"I was going to buy you a car when you graduated," he muttered, obviously flustered when she didn't fall in line after his none-too-subtle threat.

"Keep the car. I don't need it. You're always dangling the carrot, aren't you? I've lost my taste for it. What I need is a father, and since you won't be one to me, I'm going to say good night."

"So you're going to turn your back on me just like that faggot brother of yours?"

Her brother, Darren, was her best friend and to hear her father use such a derogatory term toward his own son pissed her off. "His name is Darren and he's your son. He may not be your ideal of manhood, but he knows more about being a man than you ever will. You can keep your expensive gifts. I don't want them. And please don't contact me again until you decide to get over yourself." Grabbing her purse, she stormed away from the table. As she left, she requested the maître d' call her father a cab before her dad left and if he insisted on driving, call the police. Regardless of what she felt for the man, he was still her father and she didn't want him to die doing something foolish. Not to mention, she was hopefully saving the lives of any people on the road who might cross paths with him.

She slid into the beat up economy car she'd had since high school and was annoyed when the engine didn't start right away. Her car was a long-serving hand-me-down. Her father had bought it used for her mother; then when her brother, Darren, had passed his driving test and received his license, their mom had given it to him. Later, it had become Camryn's. "Come on, old girl, don't break down on me now. We made it here from Atlanta. You can drive a half hour more to Mom's house." As if by magic, when she turned the key in the ignition again, it started. At least it was one less worry. For the moment.

Camryn was excited about seeing her mom again and thrilled at the prospect of a baby brother or sister. She was even happy at the prospect of seeing Marc, her stepfather— who also happened to be a vampire. He was actually very nice and it was clear he was crazy about her mother which is what counted most. She was still trying to adjust to the fact that her mother was now also a bloodsucker. It was difficult to believe there were beings in existence she'd been conditioned to not believe in. So far, the Grimaldi family had been nothing but kind to her but she was still wary of them mainly because she was still coming to terms with the existence of vampires and their ilk. She was almost certain none of them would hurt her but many years of monster movies and books still rested in the back of her mind. And then there was Jagger.

She still chided herself for allowing him to seduce her that day he'd come to visit her in Atlanta. She should have told him to leave her alone but instead, she'd invited him into her apartment and let him do things to her she hadn't allowed any other man to do. She still wasn't one hundred percent convinced he hadn't put a spell on her of some sort. Why else would she act so wantonly once he touched her? She'd never experienced an orgasm so explosive either and it frightened and excited her at the same time.

Admittedly, Camryn was more attracted to him than she wanted to be but Jagger was a dangerous man. It was because she was so attracted him that she needed to stay away. She had goals in life to be her own woman and maintain her independence. A man like Jagger could easily make her forget those dreams. She wasn't interested in a relationship with him or any man.

Up until the moment Jagger ate her pussy and made her scream until her throat was raw, Camryn hadn't seen the big deal about sex. The couple of boyfriends she'd had were nothing to write home about. She'd given the last guy she dated her virginity, but the sex was pretty awful. Her partner had claimed he knew what he was doing but in the end, he had left her frustrated and wondering what the big deal was. Although it should have, it didn't bother her in the least when he'd dumped her shortly after their awkward encounter in the bedroom.

Since then, Camryn had declined dates preferring the company of her vibrator if she felt the need to get off. She'd developed the reputation of being an ice queen on campus which unfortunately was a challenge to a bunch of dickheads who wouldn't take no for an answer. Often, Camryn would look at happy couples holding hands and laughing together and cynically think it wouldn't last. She'd learned a long time ago from watching her parents that she was better off without a man in her life; at least not one who would dominate and control her. If she ever did settle down, when she was much older and simply in need of companionship, it would be with a guy who wouldn't try to change her in the name of love.

Camryn didn't care for men who came on too strong, and in their very first meeting, Jagger's intense amber gaze had stamped her with stark possessiveness. At first, she hadn't known how to react, because no one had ever dared to look at her that way before, like she belonged exclusively to him. Like he wanted to consume her soul. And the crazy part was, she wasn't sure if that was a bad thing. Of course once she came to her senses, she realized how ridiculous a notion that was and immediately cast that thought aside.

Jagger was the kind of man who would expect complete servitude from his woman. He'd rule and dominate her until she was no longer herself. She didn't want to be the shell of a woman her mother had been when her parents were still together.

The thought of spending the next two weeks with her mother brought to mind another dilemma. She'd been told the rest of the Grimaldi clan would also be in residence, waiting for arrival of the baby. That meant he would be there as well. She had no idea how she could avoid him and not look at him and remember his head between her thighs and how he had occupied her dreams.

She somehow had to be strong in the days to come and focus on her mother and the new baby. If he walked into a room, she'd walk out and she'd make sure she was never alone with him. Maybe if he hadn't come to Atlanta, she could have played nice and pretended everything was okay, but he'd ruined it.

The blaring honk of a car horn brought her back to reality. Camryn realized her car had drifted to the center of the road, straddling two lanes. She immediately maneuvered the vehicle to one side and shot an apologetic hand in the air for the driver behind her. Just one more exit to her mother's house.

She whispered a silent prayer that she would make it past this visit without another encounter like the last with Jagger Grimaldi. The biggest problem was part of her wasn't sure if she wanted him to leave her alone.

Chapter Five

"Maggie, have a seat and put your feet up. Camryn should be here shortly; she called to say she'd come as soon as the dinner with her father ends."

Maggie looked out the window for the tenth time that night. No matter how old they got, she always worried about her children. "I know, but it makes me nervous to know she's still driving around in that lemon. That thing is only holding on by a hope and a prayer. Hopefully, she'll make it here without breaking down."

"If she managed to drive from Atlanta to Virginia, I'm sure she'll make the next twenty miles of her trip."

Maggie sighed. Her husband was probably right, but her concerns would not be allayed until her daughter actually walked through the door safe and sound. "I wish she hadn't refused our offer to buy her a new car. I think I'm going to have to insist when she gets here."

GianMarco stood behind Maggie, wrapping his large, sinewy arms around her waist, his hands cupping the considerable bulge of her stomach. They were expecting their first child together any day now, and Maggie couldn't remember a time when she'd been happier except for the birth of her two older children.

Her husband grazed her ear with his tongue, causing a shiver to run through her body. She leaned against his solid frame, reveling in the warmth of his body cradling hers. She'd never felt so protected and loved in her life until she met this gorgeous hunk who was now her husband. There was no feeling like knowing the love you gave was returned with equal intensity. Maggie was so in love with this man that she sometimes feared she'd wake up and this would all be a dream.

"Camryn is a very independent young woman. She probably gets that stubborn streak from her mother."

Maggie twisted around to face him, staring into his eyes. It was still hard to believe this man belonged to her and she to him. In a million years, she couldn't have guessed when her marriage of twenty-three years ended abruptly that she'd land on her feet like this.

Left with practically nothing, her self-esteem at its lowest, Maggie had found herself starting over again at the age of forty. After weeks of searching for employment, she'd been extremely fortunate to land a job as a secretary for a detective agency. Little had Maggie known, however, that her obnoxious but sexy boss was a vampire. She and GianMarco had gotten off to a rocky start, avoiding each other whenever it was possible while denying the underlying attraction that existed between them. Once they both stopped fighting their feelings for one another, there had been no turning back. Now, she had to constantly pinch herself to make sure she wasn't dreaming because every morning she woke with a smile on her face and went to bed wrapped in a pair of muscular arms.

Since she and GianMarco had married, two of her brothers-in-law had also found mates. She hoped the same could happen for Dante, the eldest Grimaldi brother. Maggie wanted him to find the same happiness she shared with GianMarco. Thinking about Dante made her slightly uncomfortable, because she felt responsible for the rift between him and GianMarco. Dante had somehow gotten it into his head that he had feelings for her which had caused a great deal of friction between the brothers. She could tell that this discord hurt GianMarco and she wished for the relationship to be repaired.

She placed her head against GianMarco's broad chest. "Do you think..."

"Do I think Dante will come?"

She nodded, not trusting herself to speak. She hadn't been a vampire for quite a year, so she was still getting used to the nuances of their kind. Mind reading was one of their talents she had yet to grow accustomed to.

"He said he'd come, but I haven't heard from him since our last conversation. The last I heard from him was a couple weeks ago—"

"That's the longest the two of you have gone without speaking to each other isn't it?" she asked gently.

GianMarco nodded. The pain was evident in his amber gaze. She cupped the side of his face with her hand. "This is all my fault."

He grasped her hand and brought it to lips. "Don't ever think that. I've already told you, you're not to blame. This is something that will sort itself out. Right now, he just needs a little time away from the family to get his head together. He's been in Greece for the past couple weeks, spending time with Paris Kyriakis and his family."

"I think you might have mentioned the Kyriakis family before. Are they the werewolves?"

GianMarco chuckled. "Yes, but don't ever let them hear you call them werewolves. It's kind of an offensive term to them. Shifters is what they prefer to be called. Paris is the Alpha of Pack Kyriakis. He and Dante have been close friends for years. Apparently, there was some kind family crisis with Paris's son and Dante was giving them a hand."

"Oh no, is he in any danger?"

"I don't think so. He would tell me if that were the case. Dante may miss the actual birth, but I'm confident he'll come back soon. Don't worry about it, *ciccina*, you are not to blame."

Maggie wanted to believe him but that twinge of guilt still remained. But she decided it was best that she not bring it back up. With a sigh, she rested her head against his chest, enjoying it being just the two of them. In a very short time, the house would be a circus of activity.

GianMarco must have felt the same way because he held her tightly against him. "Let's enjoy this quiet for a moment because the family should descend on us tomorrow."

"Oh!" Maggie smacked her forehead.

"What is it?" GianMarco's dark brows furrowed together.

"Sasha called earlier and said she, Niccolo, and Jagger would be here tonight."

"And Camryn is on the way?"

"Yes." Camryn had let slip to Maggie about her meeting with Jagger when she had last visited. But even if her daughter hadn't mentioned the encounter, it was clear Jagger was smitten with her. And it was just as evident that Camryn wasn't comfortable with the attention. From Maggie's observation, Camryn was more interested than she was willing to let on but it was a conclusion Camryn needed to come to herself. "Do you think there will be a problem with Camryn and Jagger under the same roof?"

"I don't know, *ciccina*. It should certainly be interesting, but I think there will be plenty of people in the house to keep each of them occupied. Romeo, Christine, and their children will be arriving tomorrow morning."

"It's so funny to think of Romeo as a family man now. I always thought he'd remain a bachelor forever. Now, he not only has a wife but two children." Maggie giggled.

"You're telling me. I've known him for much longer than you and trust me, I never saw it coming either but Christine and the kids make him happy so I'm happy for him."

"Me too. I'm glad they've decided to take up residence in this area. There are a lot of houses for sale around here; it will be so much fun house shopping with Christine. Our baby could use some little playmates."

GianMarco smiled indulgently before dropping a kiss on her forehead.

A rush of white pain ripped through her lower body. She doubled over. But just as quickly as it came, it was gone. Maybe she'd imagined it.

"Maggie, are you okay?"

She didn't want to alarm her husband, so she answered in the affirmative. "I'm fine. I just get a little winded sometimes is all."

He looked unconvinced. "If you're sure..."

She straightened up and pinned a smile on her face. "I am. I guess I'm just anxious to see Camryn."

"She'll be here soon. In the meantime, I have an idea how to take your mind off of things."

She raised a brow, liking where this was going. "Does it have anything to do with making love?"

A large lopsided grin split his face. "You know me so well."

At that moment something happened to cancel any chances of them making it to the bed. "I would love to, but I don't think it's a good idea."

He knitted his brows. "Why not? You've never been one to turn down our lovemaking."

"And you know I enjoy it immensely, but my water just broke."

Chapter Six

"It's okay, Uncle Marco. I'll let Camryn know what's happened as soon as she arrives," Jagger assured the older vampire.

GianMarco who was understandably distracted merely nodded as he ran around the house making sure everything was in order. Maggie seemed to be handling the situation much better. "Baby, calm down. Everything will be fine. This isn't my first time having a baby. There's nothing to be nervous about," she assured her husband.

Niccolo patted Maggie on the shoulder. "You must indulge my brother in his panic; after all, he hasn't been a father for many centuries. Besides, this is your first child together so naturally this will be a very special event for the both of you."

Maggie sighed. "I understand but if we don't get out of here soon, I'll end up having the baby right here in the living room since we have an hour's drive ahead of us. I doubt everyone wants to see that spectacle. And, I think GianMarco is too much of a wreck to drive us to the hospital."

"Which is why Sasha and I will come with you two," Niccolo said.

Finally, GianMarco slowed down and moved to his wife's side. "You're right, Maggie but as my brother pointed out, I don't want anything to go wrong. When my son was born, we didn't have the modern conveniences of today so I'm sure everything will go off without a hitch."

Maggie rubbed her protruding belly with a smile. "Of course it will. Besides, I'm a vampire now. I'll heal pretty quickly as you've already pointed out."

GianMarco nodded. "You will, but I also told you, you'd lose a lot of blood. You'll be weak for at least a couple days."

"I still don't see why I can't have the baby at home. I'll be just fine."

"Because this particular hospital caters to our kind and I want you to have as stress-free an experience as possible."

"Well, now that you two have that settled, I think we should go," Niccolo ushered them toward the door. "Go ahead and I'll be out in a minute." Once the others left the house, Niccolo turned to face his son. His expression was serious and Jagger wasn't sure if he'd like what his father had to say.

"I won't ask you if you'll be alright alone because I know you will. You mother has placed wards on the house so no one uninvited can get in. And there are Underground agents around who will be on the lookout for any suspicious activity."

"I know, Papa. You forget I'm an adult and capable of taking care of myself."

Niccolo nodded. "Of course, but we're not dealing with ordinary circumstances here. There has already been an attack on Maggie and GianMarco by a couple of rogues so we have to be extra careful."

"I get that but I get the distinct impression my security isn't the topic you wanted to discuss."

"You're right, it isn't. From what I gathered, Camryn will arrive shortly. I know the temptation is great but you must tread lightly."

Jagger frowned at the implication of Niccolo's words. "Do you think I would take her by force?"

"Of course not I—"

"Because trust me, anything that happens between me and Camryn will be consensual."

Niccolo raised a brow. "You sound certain."

"Because I am."

"Did something physical happen when you went to Atlanta?"

Seeing no need to lie to his father, Jagger nodded. "Yes."

His father gave him a long assessing stare before commenting. "That would explain it then."

"Explain what?"

"When you came to L.A. a few weeks ago, your symptoms seemed to indicate you were on the verge of *la morte dolci*, but when you returned from Atlanta you seemed fine. Did you two consummate this thing you have? Completely, I mean?"

"Not completely, no. Does it make a difference?"

"Yes. Your symptoms will eventually return until it happens. So getting back to my original statement, tread lightly. I know you may want her badly but this is a delicate situation. Promise me, you will keep your hands to yourself until she gives you her absolute consent."

"Papa, I would never—"

Niccolo clutched Jagger's wrist. "Promise me."

"Okay. I promise."

"Good. We'll be in touch when the baby arrives."

"Of course."

Once Jagger was alone, he let out a long sigh of relief. The beginning of this visit wasn't quite turning out how he thought it would. Chaos had reigned in the household when he and his parents had arrived. They'd been greeted by his frantic uncle and exasperated aunt. Though they'd expected the baby to arrive within a few days, no one thought it would be tonight. But, it was as if some divine intervention had occurred in his favor for this to happen the way it did.

He'd be alone with Camryn and he could finally explain to her what he'd meant to in Atlanta.

During his entire plane ride here, he'd thought about little else but seeing her again. He remembered how she'd felt in his harms, how she'd screamed his name and how she'd tasted. His cock jumped to attention as he remembered how beautiful she'd looked beneath him. It was gratifying to know she was not as adverse to him as she pretended and Jagger was determined to get her to admit that she wanted him as much as he wanted her.

Jagger glanced impatiently at his watch wondering where the hell she was. It was nearly midnight. He could have sworn Maggie had told him Camryn would be here by now. He hoped she hadn't changed her mind and decided not to show up because of him. At that very moment, the loud clanging of an engine drew closer to the house. Hurrying to look out the window, Jagger could just make out the driver behind the wheel. His heart pounded in anticipation of seeing her face again.

His prick was so stiff, it strained against his pants, threatening to split them open. He had to relax and appear as non-threatening as possible. Despite what had happened in her apartment, he wasn't foolish enough to assume she'd simply fall into his arms just because he wanted her to. It was helpful that his symptoms for the onset of *la morte dolci* had abated some but not much. Unbeknownst to his father, it wasn't that his symptoms had gone away completely, he was just able to handle them better. But Jagger wasn't sure for how much longer.

He glanced out the window and was appalled that she'd driven her wreck of a car such a significant distance. It was fine for local driving, he supposed, but not from Georgia to Virginia. He made a mental note to find her a safer form of transportation. He shook his head in disgust as he watched the death trap sputter up the driveway louder than he remembered. Jagger desperately wanted to go outside and greet her but he decided his best course of action would be to let her come to him, despite wanting nothing more than to yank her out of the car and fuck her right on the ground until nothing else in the world mattered.

The car finally came to a halt, but not before releasing a menacing pop. He paced the floor waiting for her. It seemed like an hour to Jagger while he waited for her to get out of the car and reach the front door, although he knew it had to be only a couple of minutes. His heart pounded faster than ever at the sound of the doorbell. Taking a deep breath, Jagger opened the door.

Camryn took a step backward and shook her head. "No. Not you. Not tonight." Her jaw practically fell to the ground and her dark eyes widened to the size of saucers.

"Welcome, Camryn. I'm glad to see you've arrived safely, although I'm sure your car has seen better days." He moved back enough to let her by, but not enough that she could avoid brushing against him.

If possible, Camryn was even prettier than he remembered her being from their last encounter; her smooth mahogany skin was free of makeup except for a light coat of gloss on her curvy lips that smelled like strawberries. He steeled himself to not pounce and taste the sweetness of her mouth until it was bare. Unlike the last time, her hair was loose and big, like a dark fluffy cloud framing her beautiful face and resting on her shoulders. He barely managed to stop himself for reaching out and running his fingers through it.

He allowed his gaze to drift over her body and admired the way her tight yellow t-shirt hugged her breasts and skimmed her slender waist and how her jeans accentuated the curve of her hips. Though she was facing in, he could only imagine what her ass looked like in those jeans, which were begging to be torn off. Camryn had a magnificent ass. It was only after meeting Camryn, did Jagger finally understand why so many rappers paid homage to women's asses in their song lyrics. Many a night he'd lain in bed with his fist wrapped around his cock as he imagined riding her plump bottom.

"Are you finished?" she questioned with raised brows.

"Huh?" Jagger hadn't realized he'd been staring but he wasn't ashamed of showing how much he desired her.

"Are you finished staring at me? Or should I turn around so you can stare at my butt?"

Jagger grinned. "Now that you mention it…"

She rolled her eyes. "It's called sarcasm. Where is Mom and why did you answer the door?"

"And hello to you, too, beautiful."

"Please don't start."

"Start what? I was simply being polite. Do you have any bags I can bring into the house for you?"

"Don't worry about them. I can get them later."

"I insist. Why do any extra lifting if you don't need to. Give me your keys."

For a moment, she looked as if she'd refuse but finally relented. Camryn dropped the keys into his hand. Jagger headed outside, to get her belongings and used the time to get himself under control. Just being in her presence had him so hard, he wasn't sure how he'd make it through these next weeks without slamming her against a wall and taking her hard and fast.

Jagger gave himself a few extra minutes before heading back inside. He placed the bags by the door. Camryn paced the floor looking none too pleased.

"You seem anxious. Are you worried I might bite or that you'll like it?" He grinned.

"Jagger, we've discussed this already. Nothing is going to happen between us. What happened before was a mistake that won't be repeated."

"You call it a mistake, Camryn, but I think it was meant to be whether you care to admit it or not." He stepped closer until they were practically touching.

"Please, don't," she whispered.

"Don't what? Tell you the truth? That what happened actually meant something to me and I think it meant something to you, too?"

She shook her head and took several steps back. "People have meaningless sex all the time. Don't think make more of it than it actually was."

"There was nothing meaningless about what happened between us. You might deny it now, but need I remind you, how you screamed my name or how wet your pussy got? You can lie to yourself if you want, Camryn, but don't lie to me."

She looked around, anxiety seeming to take over. "Where is everyone?"

Jagger realized her abrupt change of subject was a tactic to distract him which he would allow, for now. He gestured to the sofa. "You should probably have a seat first."

"I won't sit down until you tell me what's going on. Where's Mom? Is she okay? Oh, no! Mom is okay, isn't she?"

"Your mother is fine. I suspect that in a few hours she'll be more than okay. Uncle Marco, on the other hand, I'm not so sure. He's the one in need of help, I should imagine."

Confusion washed over her face before comprehension dawned. Her voice was no more than a whisper. "The baby?"

He nodded with a smile. "Very soon your new little brother will be here."

"What makes you think it's going to be a boy? It could be a girl as well, in fact, my mother is sure of it."

Jagger shrugged. "The chances of her having a daughter are slim to none."

"Why is that? Aren't there female vampires?"

"Yes, there are, and most of them have been made rather than born."

"But there have been some who have been born right?"

"Only a handful. For some reason unknown to anyone, the X chromosome isn't produced but every so often in a vampire's sperm."

"Oh." Her disappointment was clear.

"You really wanted a little sister, didn't you?"

"I already have a brother, one I love very much, but Mom was so sure about the sex of the baby, I began to believe it, too. I was getting used to the idea. Oh, well, I'll be just as happy with a little brother. I'm glad for Mom no matter what the sex of the baby is, and for Marc, too, of course."

"Of course."

An awkward silence fell between them, the light ticking of the grandfather clock in the living room corner the only sound. Jagger couldn't tear his gaze away from her beautiful face to save his life. Camryn, on the other hand, made every attempt to look anywhere but in his direction.

"It doesn't have to be this way, you know."

She laughed nervously. "I don't know what you're talking about."

"Camryn, let's stop playing foolish games. The chemistry between us is real. What happened in Atlanta only proves it."

"I thought I made it clear I don't want to talk about that. It was an aberration on my part. Besides, I'm not completely blind to the fact that you're a very skilled lover. I'm sure you could wring that response out of a nun."

"I'm not concerned with anyone else but you." Jagger sighed with frustration. He could have insisted they talk it out right then but with the impending arrival of the baby, they had phone calls to make. "Okay, Camryn. You win for now. But this conversation is far from over. In the meantime, we need to contact friends and family and notify them of the joyous event which is about to occur. Uncle Marco left his address book and marked the people he wanted me to get in touch with. It's a pretty big list and I figure we'll get through it faster if we work together. Do you think we could call a truce for the sake of the family? After all, we will soon have another relative in common."

Warring emotions flashed within the depths of her eyes. Her gaze finally met his, making Jagger's heart skip a beat. The incredible heat he hadn't fully experienced since Atlanta resurfaced. The hot flash tore through his body but he managed to remain calm without alerting her as to what was going on within him.

Jagger licked his now dry lips, taking a step back as much for his sake as hers. The movement must have taken her by surprise because she eyed him with suspicion.

"How can I trust you?"

"You'll just have to go on faith. I promise not to touch you...unless you want me to."

"That will never happen."

Jagger smiled. "If you say so."

"I do. No funny stuff, okay?"

"How could I try anything when the rest of the family will be here by tomorrow morning?"

"Well...if you realize nothing will ever happen between us, I guess we could call a truce, but don't get any ideas."

"You don't sound like you trust me."

"With your track record it's pretty hard to."

"Well, if you recall, you were also a willing participant."

Camryn glared at him. "Don't start."

"Okay, I'll behave...to the best of my abilities. Friends?"

She seemed hesitant, probably wondering if she could accept his offer at face value. He, of course, had no intention of simply remaining her friend but friendship was at least a way for him to get himself through the metaphorical door. "I..."

His smile widened. "You want to say yes."

"Okay but you don't get to mention what happened at my place again. Okay?"

"Deal."

"You said that too quickly."

"Because, I will still have my memories."

"Jagger..."

"What?" he asked in mock confusion. "You said I wasn't allowed to talk about it. You never said anything about me thinking about it."

Camryn giggled. "You're outrageous."

Jagger chuckled enjoying this easy banter with her. It was the first time he felt he was making some actual headway, albeit small. "Do you like outrageous? I can be even more outrageous if you'd like me to be."

"No. I just want you to act normal."

"Normal is boring. But if your friendship is what you have to offer me for now, I'll take it. Shall we shake on it?"

"Don't push your luck, buddy."

Montana Donavan squealed on the other end of the phone. "She's having the baby now? Why didn't she call me earlier? I thought we were girlfriends!" Her godmother was an excitable woman; Camryn sometimes wondered how opposites like her mother, who was calm and laid back, and Montana, who was high maintenance and outspoken, had remained best friends for nearly thirty years.

"I don't think she had much of a chance. I would imagine since this is Marc's first baby after losing his son that he was so excited he rushed her off. At least, that's the version I've been told."

"Who told you? Wasn't your mother there when you arrived?"

"No. Actually, Marc's nephew, Jagger, was here. He's keeping me company, but trust me, you are the second person I called. I had to tell Darren first, of course. He's thrilled."

"So you're in the house alone with..." Montana's voice lowered several decibels, "one of them?"

"Why are you whispering?"

"Can't he hear you? They have great hearing, you know."

For as long as Camryn had known Montana, the older woman had never seemed to be afraid of anything or anyone but there was a surprising hint of fear in her voice. She wondered what had happened between Montana and the Grimaldi family to frighten her fearless godmother. "I'm aware of that, but Jagger's hauling my stuff to my room."

"You're not still driving that black hunk of junk, are you?"

"I am and it broke down on me ten minutes from the house. My cell phone battery died and I was stranded."

"How did you get there?"

"I played with some wires under the hood. This guy, I know, showed me how one of the cables keeps getting disconnected from this thingamabob. I don't know what it's called, but he told me what to do if my car stalled again. I must have done something wrong because there was a mini explosion, but I managed to reconnect the wires."

"So it did start?"

"Sort of. It made the most awful noise, coughing and sputtering the entire way here, and to top it off, it only went five miles an hour. I think my poor baby is on its last legs."

"That piece of crap has been on its last legs for the past ten years. When your father bought that car for your mother, it was already three years old. That cheap bastard could have sprung for a new ride, he certainly could have afforded it instead of spending his money on his floozies."

"Montana, even though he isn't my favorite person right now, he's still my father."

"You're right. I'm sorry. I just get so angry when I think about how that assh—he treated your mother for all those years."

"She had the option to leave but she never did." Camryn tried to inject a nonchalance into her voice that she didn't feel. Talking about her parents' marital problems was a sore spot for her. It still had the ability to make her tear up for the little girl who'd lived through the arguments, mental, and verbal abuse.

"You have to know it wasn't that simple. She believed she was making the right decision by staying. But enough about that, I just need to leave the past where it belongs, in the past. Anyway, do you want me to come over to keep you company? In case you don't want to be alone with that...with whatever he is."

"I'm fine."

"Are you sure? I know Maggie says vampires are safe, but...there's something I can't quite shake about them. Something I don't like."

"Look, I'm not exactly ecstatic my mom has become a bloodsucker, but she's happy with Marc so I'm happy for her. If I for a second thought he'd harm a hair on her head, I'd stake him through the heart.

"I guess you're right, but once when I went to visit something happened."

"What?"

"That's just it. I don't remember anything, except the color red, so it must have been horrible. I get chills when I try to force the memory. Just be careful, okay?"

"I usually am. You have nothing to worry about. I can take care of myself."

"Famous last words. You just watch yourself, young lady. Maggie tells me the Grimaldi men are great charmers."

"I can't be charmed," Camryn shot back, growing frustrated with the conversation.

"Your mother wasn't looking for anything either and the next thing I know, she's pregnant, in love, and getting married. Trust me, those men move fast. Once they decide they want you, you can pretty much count your freedom goodbye."

That's what Camryn was afraid of but she wouldn't admit it. "Like I said, I'll be fine."

When she finally hung up the phone, Camryn was struck with the decision of whether to join Jagger in the living room or run to her room and hide. Though the idea was appealing, she couldn't avoid the guy forever and she'd already made the appropriate phone calls. It was nearly one o'clock now, but she wasn't sleepy.

Pulling an elastic band from her pocket, she fixed her hair into a ponytail as she remembered how Jagger had told her he wanted to run his fingers through her hair. That wasn't going to happen if she could help it.

She found him on the couch playing solitaire on the coffee table, a look of concentration on his handsome face. She had never had the chance to study him like this when he was unaware of her. A lock of thick black hair fell over his forehead, and his profile was strong, his jaw square.

Camryn's breath caught in her throat. Jagger's looks were almost surreal. She'd only ever seen men like him in magazines and even then, she knew they were heavily photoshopped. All the Grimaldi men were incredibly good-looking but none of them affected her the way Jagger did. At that moment, she wished he wasn't so easy on the eyes.

Instinct told her to turn around and head to her room, but she remained rooted to the spot. "You can do this. You are not interested in a relationship. You don't need a man," she chanted under her breath.

Without turning away from his task, he asked, "Are you going to stand there talking to yourself or will you join me?"

She'd forgotten about his sensitive hearing. "I wasn't talking to myself."

"Oh, so I didn't hear you muttering about not needing a man? My mistake." He continued to lay cards on the table, still not bothering to glance her way.

Why his sudden lack of attention bothered her was baffling. "Okay, fine. Maybe I did say I don't need a man. It's true."

"Of course you don't," he murmured, still not turning his head in her direction. His accent was too sexy for words. Was there anything about him that wasn't hot?

Again, she had the chance to leave the room but remained in the same spot. It was as if a force she couldn't quite explain kept her from running away. She wanted to blame Jagger for putting a spell on her but deep down, Camryn knew that wasn't the case. "So, uh, what are you doing?" she asked despite knowing the answer already.

"Playing solid."

"Solid?"

"You know, the card game one plays alone."

She giggled at his mispronunciation. It was kind of cute. "I think you mean solitaire."

"*Da.* That's probably what I meant. My English gets mixed up sometimes."

Camryn took the seat on the opposite end of the couch from Jagger. "You sound as if you've been speaking it for years."

"I have, all my life, actually, although I don't use it as often as I should and I don't speak it as well as I'd like. My grandmother is English, so I learned Russian and English from the cradle. She would speak English exclusively to me but when I was around ten, she stopped coming around. I believe she and my mother didn't see eye to eye on some things and that was the end of her visits. My mother is pretty proficient with languages so I would practice my

English with her as well. It's not as good as I'd like it to be because I still mess up a word from time to time."

"What other languages do you speak?"

"Czech, French, Polish, and a smattering of German."

"That's impressive. I took five years of Spanish in high school and college but I'm nowhere near fluent."

"It's really not that remarkable. My father speaks over fifty languages and there are so many more for him to learn. I'm sure you can imagine I have a ways to go before I even catch up to him or my uncles."

"You're only thirty, right? For your age, I think you're definitely on track to pick up several more. After all, you do have an eternity to do it," she whispered, remembering he wasn't human.

"I sense your unease; there is no need to be frightened of me. I'm not so different from you."

Camryn couldn't help snorting at that comment. "Um, I'm not a bloodsucking warlock vampire, or vampire warlock. Whatever you call yourself. What do I call you anyway?"

He looked at her, then revealed a perfect white smile that made her heart flutter. "Jagger will do nicely. And I agree you're not a bloodsucker, as you so quaintly put it. You're a beautiful young woman—and an extremely desirable one, at that, but as I was saying, you shouldn't judge immortals so harshly without getting to know us."

"You suck blood and have magical powers. What else is there to understand?"

He laid the deck of cards down. Sweat broke out on her forehead, when she noticed his muscular hands flex and stretch.

"Can I ask you a question without you becoming offended?" His gaze bore into her.

"It depends on what the question is."

"Okay, answer me this: do you always make judgments about people you barely know without getting to know them or does that particular honor just belong to me?"

His question threw Camryn for a loop. "Of course not. I try to give everyone I meet a fair chance."

"Yet from the moment we met, you've been hostile toward me and I don't believe I deserved it."

"You were stalking me! How else was I supposed to act?"

"That excuse would actually be valid if you weren't that way at our first meeting and as for the stalking, I admit that I visited your school twice, once without your knowledge. By the way, the first time, was simply to see you and nothing more. I couldn't stop thinking about you so I wanted to know for certain if I had imagined the instant attraction I felt toward you. I saw you on campus, watched you have lunch with a couple friends and that was it. Afterwards, I left. The second time, I revealed myself so if you want to call me a stalker fine, but you don't get to use that as an excuse to describe your passive aggressive attitude toward me."

Camryn opened her mouth to refute his statement but Jagger wasn't finished.

"And you make disparaging remarks about my heritage."

"How and when have I done that?"

"You don't think calling me a bloodsucker marginalizes who I am as a person? Trust me Camryn. I'm much more than that. I'm not easily offended and the word itself doesn't bother me but the vehemence you use behind it does. I bet you'd be surprised to know, I've only ingested blood only once in my entire existence."

By now, she was mortified that she had somehow offended him by throwing words around so carelessly. She was no stranger to discrimination and it sickened her that she could be that way toward anyone else. She cupped her flaming cheeks as she looked away from the intensity of his stare. "I didn't know. This is pretty embarrassing."

He scooted closer to her on the couch and gently placed his hand on her knee. An electric current tore through her body at that slight contact. Before she could move away from his touch, Jagger removed his hand first. "Camryn my goal isn't to embarrass you but to get you to see me. There are bad warlocks, shifters, and vampires out there and, they're a threat to all of us. But just as there are bad immortals, there are bad humans. Yes, I'm a vampire-warlock hybrid but that's not all I am. I'm a man who saw a woman I felt an instant connection to and whether you believe it or not, you're more of a danger to me than I am to you."

"Now you're pulling my leg," she muttered still too afraid to make eye contact.

"Look at me, Camryn."

She shook her head.

"Please." Even though he'd asked politely, the command still remained in his tone.

Slowly, she raised her head and gasped at the naked and unabashed lust in his amber gaze. Camryn couldn't move if she wanted to. It seemed like the more she tried to fight the attraction between the two of them, she found herself even more drawn to him.

"You have the power to hurt me more than you can know, Camryn. I know you're not ready to hear this yet, but I have feelings for you and I think you may feel the same way. And before you use the short span of our acquaintance as an excuse, my heart doesn't need forever to know how I feel. I respect that you still have to come to terms with those feelings and that's fine, but don't use my being immortal as shield for your hang-ups. I think it's best if I go to another part of the house before I do something like break my promise to my father."

Camryn wasn't sure what that last part meant but she felt like a first-class jerk. Though he hadn't come right and said it, she'd hurt him. She didn't want to be the source of anyone's pain, let alone someone who'd just poured their heart out to her. When Jagger stood to leave, she grabbed his wrist. "You don't have to go."

A half smile curved his lips. "I think I do. I'm not sure I can trust myself around you without a repeat of Atlanta."

There was a flutter in the pit of her stomach as she remembered that day. The scary part was, even if he did make an advance toward her, she wasn't sure she'd stop him. "Okay, but...I wanted to apologize. I'm sorry. I didn't mean to come off as ignorant in my comments. You're right, they were offhand and I didn't think."

"Camryn, I don't want you to apologize, but if you have any questions about my being a vampire, I'd rather you asked instead of making blanket assumptions based on what you might have seen in a movie or read in a book. Deal?"

She nodded. "Whether you want my apology or not, you have it. Before my mom settled down with Marc, I had no idea vampires and other immortals existed, and the media has always portrayed them as monsters, but Marc has been good to my mom and my brother and me. All the Grimaldi's have been kind and I've...I've been stand-offish because..." It was hard to verbalize something she didn't fully comprehend herself.

He nodded. "We'll talk about this another time, Camryn. Just think about what I said, okay? I have a few more calls to make. Get some rest."

She laughed half-heartedly. "I don't think I'll be able to sleep until I hear news on my mom."

"Okay. Goodnight Camryn."

"Goodnight Jagger."

Jagger was halfway across the room when he turned around and stalked back toward her. With a low growl, he yanked her off the couch and into his arms. Camryn barely had a chance to register what was happening before his lips were on hers.

Unlike the first time they kissed, her initial reaction wasn't to push him away. Instead, Camryn melted against the hard wall of his chest. She parted her lips, granting entrance to his probing tongue. He cupped her head in his palms, holding it steady as he devoured her. Fire licked along every nerve ending in her body. Her thighs quivered and her breasts grew painfully sensitive from being pressed against his body. She ached deep within her core.

Though Jagger had claimed he'd never use his powers on her, every time they touched was like magic. Camryn pushed her tongue forward to meet his. His taste was so thoroughly male, titillating all her senses. Much to her chagrin, Jagger was the one to pull away first, his breathing ragged.

"I'm sorry I shouldn't have done that. Goodnight, Camryn." He was gone before she could respond.

She touched her lips almost uncertain that it had happened; her skin still tingled.

There was no denying that her body wanted him. But by all costs, she had to guard her heart, though she wondered if she was fighting a losing battle.

Chapter Seven

Jagger tossed the covers off his body unable to get comfortable despite the cool blast of the central air. He couldn't stay cool no matter what he tried. Already he had stripped away the last article of his clothing, but the heat was still unbearable. His cock, rock hard and throbbing, ached like never before. There was no doubt in his mind that the symptoms of *la morte dolci* were back and this time stronger than before. It had been a mistake to steal that kiss from Camryn but she'd looked so tempting he couldn't help himself. Now, he was paying the consequences.

He wasn't sure if using his powers would do him any good but he had no other alternative. Jagger first attempted a cooling spell. It did nothing. His next attempt was a healing spell. It managed to intensify the heat. His incisors descended and he was unable to retract him. His only remaining option was to take a cold shower. Sitting up, he listened for any movement in the house. Camryn had retired to her room shortly after he'd turned in, but he wasn't sure if she was sleeping. They had yet to hear any news on his aunt's condition.

He climbed out of bed, allowing his feet to touch the cool hardwood floor. His room was one of the few without its own bathroom, so he carefully made his way down the hallway and slid into the shower stall, turning the water to its coldest setting. He sighed as the icy spray beat on his heated skin, providing him some relief."

Finally, his incisors retreated back into his gums but his cock, however, remained erect. Placing a hand against the wall, he grasped his dick, sliding his fist along the hard length. God, he hurt. Though the chilly water coupled with his masturbatory motions afforded him a little release from his pain, Jagger suspected complete satisfaction would not come until he was buried deep inside Camryn's wet pussy. He thought about how it would fit snugly around his dick while she alternately whispered and screamed his name until her throat was raw.

Jagger closed his eyes, groaning, imagining Camryn's hand sliding along his swollen shaft instead of his own. And once he fucked her senseless, he'd feast on her wet pussy until she came over and over again. He'd run his tongue over every inch of her body, leaving no part unexplored. Jagger would then flip her over on her stomach and thrust into her again as he pulled her hair.

He thought of taking her in every conceivable position that existed as he frantically pumped his cock. Remembering how beautifully responsive she'd been in his arms and her neatly trimmed pussy was enough to send him hurtling toward his peak. He grunted and groaned, unable to hold back. "Camryn," he whispered.

His seed shot from his dick, spraying the shower stall, his body shuddering uncontrollably. His breathing was ragged. Resting his head on the wall, Jagger attempted to calm down when a knock fell on the bathroom door.

Jagger raised his head in alarm. "I'll be out in a minute," he shouted.

"Are you okay? You've been in there for a long time."

A groan escaped his lips before he could stop it. "*Da.* I'm fine," he replied grateful his cock had softened, enabling him to think straight.

There was silence for a moment before she replied. "Are you sure? I heard you crying out earlier. I was just wondering if you'd hurt yourself."

This sudden interest in his wellbeing was sweet but ill-timed. "I'm okay, Camryn. I just need some privacy," he managed to bite out. His incisors descended again and his cock stirred. Just being outside the bathroom door, she was sending him back into a tailspin of fire and pain. He had to get rid of her or else he wouldn't be able to control what happened next.

"Well, if you need any help—"

"For God's sake, Camryn, would you just go away!" Jagger hadn't meant for his words to come out so harshly, but it was for her own good. No response followed and he hoped he hadn't messed up the tentative truce they'd formed. He'd apologize later, but for now he had to get himself under control.

It took several more moments until the ache within him was at least bearable and he had a handle of his bodily functions.

Finally being able to think clearly, he attempted a winter spell again. It was mainly for lowering the temperature within a small radius. He targeted himself and hoped that it worked. This time he was met with success. "Ah, much better," he sighed.

He had a feeling, however, that his spells wouldn't work for much longer. There was no telling what would have happened if Camryn had decided to poke her head in the bathroom to check in on him. He probably would have taken her right there on the floor or pulled her into the shower with him.

Turning off the shower, Jagger cursed when he noticed a thin sheet of ice on the bathroom floor. Icicles clung to the ceiling, yet he didn't feel the chill as he should have. Standing as still as possible, he allowed himself to take in the effect of his surroundings for a few minutes before toweling himself dry.

Jagger wrapped the towel loosely around his waist, then stepped into the hallway. He said a quick chant to return the bathroom back to its previous state. Heading back to his room, he became aware of being watched. He turned to see Camryn with eyes wide and mouth ajar. She was obviously returning from downstairs. When he shifted, the towel fell to his feet. He stood before her in all his naked glory, unashamed of his body.

Camryn's gaze zeroed in on his genital region. Once again his cock hardened and elongated. From the way she ogled at him, Jagger could tell she liked what she saw. The hungry gleam in her eyes said it all.

When moments passed and she still didn't move except to dampen her lips with her pretty pink tongue, Jagger's only choice was to go back to his room and quick. She might want him but he vowed he wouldn't take her until she was fully aware of all that was involved. Because once he took her, she was his. Forever. Bending down, he picked up his towel and wrapped it around his waist again, tighter this time.

"I'm sorry I snapped at you," he apologized stepping toward his bedroom as he spoke.

"Uh, it's okay. I was waiting to tell you that I'd heard from Marc. He said Mom was still in labor and the baby wouldn't arrive until later this morning or early afternoon."

"But everything is all right otherwise?"

"Yes."

"Good. I'll see you later. Sleep tight." Turning on his heel, he hurried back to his room and quickly closed the door behind him, a smile on his face. There was no more speculation. Camryn wanted him no matter how much she might deny it. A seed had been planted; he was one step closer to claiming his woman.

Camryn found it difficult to get to sleep. She was already wired, from wondering what her mom was going on with her mother but mostly, she couldn't get the image of Jagger's naked body out of her mind, from his smattering of dark hair covering a toned chest, to his washboard abs. And his cock. It was pretty impressive in size. Nestled between two muscular thighs, it was thick and long. She'd been unable to tear her gaze away from it.

She'd never experienced such a visceral reaction to a naked man before. She'd had sex before, but it was more so to find out what all her girlfriends had constantly bragged about. Her lover had had a nice build as well, but it couldn't compare to Jagger's. And he hadn't been able to get her to come as hard as Jagger had either. If she wasn't careful, she'd end up a slave to her desire for him. The first rays of sunlight streamed through the blinds in her room. She picked up her phone to see what time it was. Quarter to five and she hadn't had a wink of sleep. She doubted she could. She wanted someone to talk to but she couldn't go to Jagger because of her fear of doing something foolish in his presence.

She pulled up her contact list on her phone and selected his name. He was usually up early in the morning to go for a run. The phone rang several times before going to voicemail. With a sigh, she was about to return the phone to the nightstand when it rang.

"Hey Darren. Have you gone for your run yet?"

"No, but I was actually heading out the door to do just that. What's up, sis? Any news on Mom?"

"No. Not yet. I was just—I was just calling to talk."

"Is something the matter?"

"What makes you think something is wrong?"

"I know you, Cam, and you're not a morning person. You once threw a shoe at my head for waking you too early, although it was almost noon on a Saturday. You were like the only kid in the country who didn't want to get up early to watch cartoons."

Camryn giggled. "There's nothing wrong with preferring sleep."

"There isn't but knowing you'd rather sleep in when you can, something must be going on for you to call me this early."

"I had dinner with Dad last night."

There was a pause on the other end of the line. She knew things were strained between her brother and father since Darren had come out. Their father couldn't accept that his son was not his ideal of masculinity. Darren had basically told their father to fuck off. The two men were now at an impasse.

"Are you still there?"

"Yeah?"

"It's okay to ask about him. I know you two don't see eye to eye and he doesn't deserve to have a great son like you, but I know you still care about him."

"Of course I do. I'll always care because he's my father. It doesn't mean I have to like the guy. Did you two at least have a pleasant meal?"

"Not really. Actually, it got so contentious that Dad says he's not going to pay anymore of my school bills. Or at least, I think he did. Who knows if he meant it or not because he practically drank an entire bottle of wine by himself."

"Will you be okay? Financially, I mean. I can send you something, if you need it."

"I'll be okay. I only have one semester left to pay for and I can increase my work hours. Also, one of my professors is looking for a TA. I may look into doing that."

"Well, if you need anything—"

"I'll be fine, Darren, don't worry about me." She loved that her brother always looked out for her. Ever since they were kids, he protected her from the bigger kids and he never argued whenever their mother would ask if Camryn could tag along with him and his friends. He was the one to teach her how to ride a bike and skateboard. He was the best big brother a girl could ask for.

"So, what happened to make you think Dad is cutting you off?"

"Well, basically, he spent the entire meal badmouthing mom."

"Well, what do you expect? He's a bitter man. Mom was more woman than he deserved and he didn't treat her right. He thought she'd be waiting around to take him back but the joke was on him."

"Exactly right." She decided to leave out the part of the conversation when he'd made that nasty comment about Darren. There was no point in causing her brother any unnecessary hurt. "There are times when I don't understand how Mom could have stayed with him all those years. He ruled her and made her unhappy."

"True, but she's happy now and that's the most important thing." He paused for a moment. "Something else is bothering you, isn't it?"

"You know me so well."

"I told you I did." He chuckled.

She sighed. "Remember when I told you about Marc's nephew, Jagger?"

"The Russian hunk?"

"I never said anything about him being a hunk."

"But you did mention he was Russian and it doesn't take a genius to figure out he's a hunk. I've seen those Grimaldi men and there's not a single one who isn't drop dead gorgeous. Every time, I come home from visiting Mom, Bryan asks me twenty questions because he's convinced I'm going to run off with one of them." He laughed out loud.

"I didn't realize Bryan was the jealous type."

"He isn't but the Grimaldi men would make any red blooded male a little envious. So what's going on with Jagger?"

Camryn filled Darren in on her encounters with Jagger, leaving out the more intimate details. Once she was done, she asked, "So what do you think?"

"I think you have it bad."

"I don't know how I feel."

"Cam, since you've been allowed to date, you've been keeping men at arm's length. Whenever you did go out with a guy, there didn't seem to be any chemistry. For a while, I was starting to wonder if you were gay too but then I realized it was something much deeper."

"What are you talking about?"

"Not all men are like Dad. It's okay to let go and give in to your feelings. That's the beauty about love. Sometimes it works out and sometimes it doesn't but when you're in it, it's the most amazing feeling in the world. Don't use our parent's relationship as a measuring stick for the rest of your life."

"But it's not just that," she protested. "I've got dreams. I want to have a career and travel the world. I want to visit all fifty states. I want to ride a mule down the side of the Grand Canyon."

Something she said must have struck him as hilarious because Darren burst into laughter.

"What's so funny?"

"You're kidding right? About the mule part?"

"Of course not. Isn't that what people do when they visit the Grand Canyon?"

"Yeah, the lunatics who have a death wish."

"My point is, I want my life to be my own, to come and go as I please without being accountable to anyone."

"Who says you can't do all the things you want and be in a relationship? The best part of being with someone is being able to do things together and if you have dreams, the person you're with will support you. Are you scared because you don't think Jagger can be that guy or because you think he can be?"

"I'm not even sure if that makes any sense."

He sighed. "Cam, my one piece of advice to you would be if it feels right in your heart and it doesn't hurt anyone else, go for it. Look, I have to go on my run now but call me as soon as you hear any word on Mom."

"Sure. Love you."

"Love you, too."

Once she ended her call, she fell back against her pillow feeling more confused than ever. She supposed what he said made sense but it was hard to determine what her true feelings were when she'd never felt this way before. The only thing she knew for certain was that she was physically and sexually attracted to him, but a relationship needed more than that to thrive.

What the hell was wrong with her anyway? She had no business thinking along those lines. There was no room in her life for any man, and that was that. When she saw Jagger again in the morning, she'd treat him cordially, but that was it. She'd pretend nothing had happened and she hadn't ogled him like a damned lecher.

Deciding it was pointless to remain in bed when she had no chance of falling asleep, she rolled off. Digging through her suitcase, she pulled out a pair of sweatpants, a t-shirt and her sneakers. Camryn hoped a walk would clear her mind. When she left her bedroom, thankfully she saw no sign of Jagger roaming around the house.

Camryn walked a couple miles and, still hadn't come to a concrete conclusion about her feelings for Jagger. She wanted to believe that he wouldn't be the kind of man to squash her dreams and keep her tethered to home and family while he did as he pleased and cheated. They all cheated. That was how she perceived things. Though she was too embarrassed to admit it, every single one of her relationships had ended badly with either the guy calling her something hurtful, frigid being one of her favorites, cold, or just plain old bitch. By her sophomore year in college, she shunned all relationships choosing to focus on her. She figured she simply wasn't cut out for romance, not that any of those guys had made her heart beat fast or her pulse race like she'd read love was supposed to.

Besides, she'd never had a good example of what a loving couple was except what was on television and she knew that was just a fantasy. From an early age, she knew something wasn't right in her household. Her father was constantly talking down to her mother. He often went as far as calling Maggie an idiot or a moron right in front of her and Darren when he felt like she'd done something wrong.

There were many times when Camryn spotted the sadness in her mother's eyes when she didn't think anyone was watching. And then, there were the women. After a while, her father made no secret of the fact that he saw other women while telling Maggie it was her fault for being out of shape and stupid. One woman had had the audacity to show up at their house once demanding to see Eugene.

Unfortunately, that wasn't the worst memory of her parents. She'd never forget it. It was shortly into her senior year in high school when she'd witnessed her father completely crush her mother's spirit. Camryn was supposed to go to a movie with friends, but one of them had gotten sick so they decided to reschedule for another time. Camryn had come home earlier than expected.

Camryn was relieved when no one was in the living room when she arrived home. She wasn't in the mood to get the third degree. After getting something to drink and fixing a snack, she headed to her room. She had to go past her parent's bedroom to get to hers.

"Who the fuck do you think you're talking to?" Her father's deafening scream halted Camryn in her tracks.

"You made a promise to me when we got married that I could eventually go back to school and follow my dreams, too. I broke my back working two jobs to help put you through college and law school, while I was pregnant. I stayed home and raised the children. Every time I mention taking a few college courses, you have some excuse about it not being the right time. What better time than now? Camryn is going away to college next year, Darren is already gone. I'd like to pursue a career, too."

"Isn't selling your baked goods at that little farmer's market enough for you? Damn, what the hell do you want from me?"

"That's just a little something I started to make a little spending money because you don't seem to think I deserve any."

"Why should you have any? I pay all the damn bills around here while you sit on your fat ass."

"I cook, clean, take your suits to the laundry mat, and wash your funky ass drawers, so I do far more around this house than you. You haven't picked up after yourself in

years. I supported you and now, it's your turn to help me earn my education."

"Bitch, you've lost your goddamn mind if you think I'd waste my money sending you to college. You're lucky you managed to marry a driven guy like me, because you're not smart enough to go to college. Not everyone is cut out for higher education and that means you. It's time you learned a few home truths. Even if by some miracle you earned a degree, who would hire you? Do you think employers just care about whether you can do the job? Not anymore. This is a beauty obsessed world and employers are looking for people to represent their brand. No one is going to want a fat middle-aged woman. Be thankful with what you have."

Camryn couldn't move if she wanted to. She'd heard her father say cruel things to her mother before but what he'd just said was way below the belt.

"What? You're going to cry now?" he continued. "You really are pathetic. I should have listened to my mother when she told me not to marry you."

Just then her father came storming out of the room as if he were the injured party instead of the other way around.

He halted upon seeing Camryn standing there. She was shaking with rage.

"Word of advice. Don't end up like your mother." That was it. There was no sense of remorse of what he probably knew she'd overheard. Instead, those cold words as he brushed passed her and headed down the stairs.

With the door still ajar, Camryn had a good view inside the master bedroom suit. Her mother sat on the edge of the bed, her face in her hands. Her shoulders trembled from her silent sobs.

Camryn wanted to go in the room and demand her mother go downstairs and tell her father off. Tell him she'd be fine on her own. Leave him. But she knew it would be pointless. Her mother would stay.

And she'd never ever forgotten that advice from her father. She never wanted to be trapped in a relationship with someone to the point where she felt helpless and had no options. Sure her parents had a miserable marriage but they had to have loved each other at some point. She'd seen the old pictures where her father had stared at her mother lovingly, and her mother had returned that look. They had smiled and laughed and loved once. But where did it all go wrong? When had her father started to feel like his wife had become a burden? At what point did her mother start feeling trapped and hopeless?

Sure she could fall for Jagger but then what? What happened when it turned bad? She didn't think she was strong enough to survive the emotional pain her mother suffered through.

Camryn was so deep in thought that when a voice interrupted her silent musings she nearly jumped out of her skin. "Such a pretty girl. Why do you look so sad?"

She hadn't noticed anyone walking along the sidewalk when she'd left the house but she hadn't really been paying attention.

The smiling red-haired woman seemed harmless enough but there was something off about her. Camyrn couldn't quite put her finger on what it was.

"Uh, I just have a lot on my mind. You have a good morning." Camryn attempted to maneuver around the woman and continue on her way but as she moved, so did the redhead.

"Excuse me," Camryn spoke as politely as she could but the woman would not let her pass.

"I'm sorry to bother you when it seems you want to be alone, but I couldn't help but notice the frown on your face. Won't you tell me about it?" The woman spoke with a heavy accent Camryn couldn't place. She didn't seem crazy but again, Camryn couldn't shake the bad vibe she got from the woman.

"Um, I'm good actually. And as you've pointed out, I'd like to be alone. Thank you for your concern though."

"Oh, I see. It's just that you look so familiar, like one of my neighbors."

"Oh?"

"Yes, Maggie?" The statement almost came out like a question as if to test Camryn's knowledge. It then occurred to Camryn that this woman could be a part of a neighborhood watch program. Being that this area had a lot of high end homes, it made sense. This woman was probably being nosey.

"How do you know my mother?"

Jagger

A smile that didn't quite reach the woman's eyes curved her lips. "I've met her. So you are her daughter. I see the resemblance. And I'm guessing you are staying with your mother and stepfather for a time, yes?"

Camryn took a step back. She was literally repulsed by this strange woman and she couldn't understand why. "Yes." She hadn't meant to volunteer that information but the word just tumbled from her lips as if it were yanked out.

"How long will you be with them?"

"A few weeks. I…" She bit her inner lip to stop herself from talking, but again, it was as if she couldn't help herself. "I'm helping her with the baby."

The redhead's green eyes gleamed with what seemed like delight. "Oh, how wonderful. I should like to see this baby. I'm sure I will eventually." Before Camryn could respond, the stranger grasped her hand and leaned close until their faces nearly touched. "If I come by…invite me in," she whispered.

Camryn yanked her hand away. "I have to go." She turned on her heels and started to run. She wasn't sure why she ran because the woman didn't chase her, all she knew was she needed to get away.

When she happened to glance over her shoulder, the woman was gone.

Chapter Eight

Camryn was out of breath by the time she made it back to the house but the odd part was, she couldn't remember what she'd been running from. The last thing she remembered was agonizing over her feelings for Jagger and then, she'd started running.

"I was wondering where you'd gotten off to. If you wanted to take a walk, I would have gone with you." Jagger appeared in the hallway as she entered the house. As if sensing something was the matter when he saw her, he asked, "Is everything okay? Did anything happen?"

She shook her head, still trying to figure out why she felt as if she'd witnessed something scary but couldn't figure out what it was. "I don't know."

"What do you mean?"

"I just don't know. I took a walk to clear my head and I just started running. It's probably nothing." She waved her hand dismissively.

He gave her a long accessing look. "You don't look like it was nothing. Let me fix you something to drink. Have a seat and I'll be with you shortly."

She nodded. It barely registered that a few weeks ago had he given her a command of any sort, she would have done her best to defy it but she was way too rattled to argue. Camryn plopped on the couch and wrapped her arms around her body. She couldn't shake the chill she felt running through her body.

As promised, Jagger returned holding a tall glass of something bright red. She eyed him suspiciously. He chuckled. "Calm down. It's just cranberry juice. Drink up."

She took the glass with shaking hands and took a few small sips before guzzling the rest down. "Thank you. I needed that." Camryn set the empty glass on the coffee table.

"You're shivering. You should have worn a jacket." He slid next to Camryn and placed his arm around her. With her settled against him, he ran his hands along the side of her arms. The motion brought heat to her chilled skin. "You really are cold. I could do a warming spell on you, if you'd like."

"Um, no thank you. I'd prefer to warm up the old fashion way. Maybe, I just had a cold flash."

Jagger raised a dark brow. Is there such a thing as a cold flash?"

Camryn shrugged. "People have hot flashes, why not cold ones."

He chuckled. "I suppose anything is possible."

His touch was driving her crazy. Slowly, heat ebbed through her body and she decided to direct the conversation to something neutral before her thoughts could take a carnal turn. "It's past eight in the morning and no one has called to update us on my mother's status. I know labor can occur for hours, but I kind of thought with her being a vampire and all, the process would be a bit smoother."

"I'm no expert on the subject but from my understanding, it's not so easy to birth a vampire child because of how draining it is to both the mother's body and the baby."

"Draining? Don't immortals have super healing power and are incapable of dying?"

"Immortals do die, just not by natural causes. And I didn't say she would die, just that it is a physically tasking experience for the mother. Vampire babies need to feed constantly once they're formed in the womb, not just on the nutrients the mother ingests, but on her blood. Once your mother gives birth, the baby must have first blood, usually from the mother and babies require nearly their weight in it. Sometimes, the baby can take enough blood to put the mother into a light coma-like sleep for several hours. It depends."

Camryn tried not to wince as she imagined a baby with fangs sucking on her mother's neck. "Yikes."

"It's okay. It's a beautiful experience from what I hear."

Camryn crinkled her nose. "Well, if that's the case, I'm glad I'm not at the hospital. I suppose you drained your poor mom dry, didn't you?"

"Actually, I didn't. I'm half warlock remember? Though first blood was necessary for me, I didn't have my first taste until this year."

"Really? Who did you drink from?"

"Feed. From my father. Actually, it's really not the blood we're interested in. It's what's in the blood that we want. It's life essence. It sustains a vampire and makes them strong."

"Life essence? And it's only found in blood?"

"It's also in...I'm not sure how to put this delicately but, it's in, how do you say, seminal fluids—male and female ejaculate."

Camryn narrowed her eyes and glared at him. "You're making that up."

"It's true. Ask any vampire and they will tell you this is true. Why do you think I enjoyed eating your delectable pussy? It's why vampires are such sexual creatures." He ran his tongue over his full bottom lip sending the clear message that he wanted to do it again.

Camryn felt her nipples stiffen and her core grew hot. If she didn't put some distance between them, she'd end up doing something she'd regret. "I'm feeling warmer already. You can let go of me now."

He grinned showing off his perfect white teeth. "What if I don't want to let you go? I rather enjoy holding you like this without you fighting me." His smile was so disarming it was hard to think.

She wiggled out of his grasp and stood up. She refused to give in to him this easily when her feelings toward him remained unclear. "Look, we've talked about this Jagger. You and I aren't happening. Why can't you accept that?"

"It's not that I can't accept it. I could accept it, if my heart didn't tell me you were the one. So, it's not a matter of me being unable to accept it. It's that I simply won't."

Why did he have to be so persistent? "Look, Jagger, maybe you think you have feelings for me but I doubt you do. There's no denying you're an extremely good looking man so you must have tons of women throwing themselves at your regularly. I doubt you ever heard the word no from a woman and that's what you find so intriguing about me. You just see me as a challenge."

Jagger stood and closed the gap between them. "A challenge is climbing Mount Everest or swimming the length of the English Channel. You are not a challenge to me. You're a woman whom I know I want to spend the rest of eternity with."

She gasped. He'd never said that before. His declaration just made her conundrum one hundred times worse. Jagger wasn't simply talking about dating and getting to know each other, he was talking forever. "Why did you have to say that?"

"Say what, Camryn? That I want to be with you? That I don't see you as just a convenient fuck? You're much more special to me than that. I've known it since we first met and perhaps I shouldn't tell you this so shortly after meeting you, but I know you're the one for me. When an immortal finds their mate, they know."

"Mate? You've got to me joking."

"I would never joke about so serious a matter."

She backed away from him. "I've already told you I'm not interested in any kind of involvement. I have dreams and goals I'd like to accomplish."

"And I'd like you to live those dreams and accomplish those goals. I just ask that I be by your side while you pursue them."

She shook her head. "You would hurt me. And I can't live with that fear hanging over my head."

"What are you talking about, *milaya moya*? What are you so afraid of?"

She practically crumbled on the inside when he spoke Russian to her. His accent alone was enough to make her want to drop her panties, but when he spoke in his native tongue, she didn't stand much of a chance. "Don't make this situation any harder than it has to be and what does that mean anyway?"

"*Milaya moya?*"

Camryn nodded.

"It means my sweet. Or sweetheart. It's an endearment."

"Well, I wish you wouldn't call me that."

Would you prefer to hear it in English? Although, I must say English isn't nearly as passionate or hot blooded as Russian. Such a cold language, English."

"No," she whispered. Why couldn't she tear her eyes away from his mouth?

"No, you wouldn't prefer me to say it in English?"

"No. I'd prefer it if you just call me Camryn."

"But that's not fun."

"But, it's what I want. I need you to understand that nothing can happen between us beyond friendship. Okay?"

"You're kidding yourself if you think we could simply be friends when I still clearly remember the taste of you on my tongue."

"Stop reminding me of that!"

"Why? It happened. And, you know what? It's going to happen again. I believe I know what your problem is."

She rolled her eyes skyward. He had to be joking. "My problem?" The guy had a huge set of balls. The nerve of him to tell *her* she had a problem.

"*Da.* Your problem. Last night you enjoyed watching me. I even suspect you didn't really knock on the bathroom door while I was showering out of some noble sense of concern. You wanted me. In a moment of clarity, you realized how much you wanted me. But now in the light of morning, you've decided to fight those feelings once again."

"No!" Camryn denied vehemently despite knowing he'd hit the nail on the head. He stalked toward her like a lazy jungle cat, his intense amber gaze holding her mesmerized. Her muscles stiffened and locked as Jagger stopped in front of her. "And you know what?"

Camryn shook her head, not trusting herself to speak.

"I enjoyed you watching me. This is what you do to my body whenever you're near." Taking her hand in his, he slid it down the length of his torso, letting her fingers glide over his solid abdomen. Camryn tried to pull her hand away when he pushed it lower, but Jagger's grip tightened. His gaze never left her face, the intensity of his stare making her quiver. Camryn gasped when her hand encountered the hard bulge in his pants.

"It's okay. *Milaya moya.* Touch me. I know you want to."

She should have walked away right then and there, but she found she could do nothing but explore the outline his cock made against his jeans.

It was just as long and thick as she remembered it being. Camryn didn't miss the sharp intake of breath Jagger made.

"You drive me crazy, woman. I have dreamed of you touching me this way and of this." He captured her face between his hands, bringing their lips together. This was the kiss she'd fantasized about all last night. She hesitated for the briefest moment before she twined her arms around his neck, pushing her body against his.

A stirring in her pussy like never before sent heat waves of delight through her body. When his tongue thrust past her lips, Camryn thought she'd lose her mind. His taste was raw, wild, and so very male. He dominated the embrace, seeking and conquering, sweeping over every recess of her mouth. Camryn's breasts puckered against the hard wall of his chest. She could never have imagined that the simple touch of their lips crushed against each other could elicit such burning desire.

Before she realized what was happening, Jagger lifted her and carried her to the kitchen table, their mouths never parting. She had no idea what he had in mind, nor did she care. She was completely and utterly lost. Emboldened, her own tongue slid out tentatively, meeting his, but Jagger seemed to have other ideas.

He pushed her back onto the table until she rested on her elbows, then dropped to his knees in front of her—but not before revealing glowing amber eyes. Camryn should have been frightened, but she was so dazed with lust, it didn't quite register. "What are you going to do?" Was that breathy whisper of a woman in the throes of passion her?

"I'm going to do something I've been dying to do to you again, since I had my first taste." Jagger yanked her sweats off and pushed her legs apart before burying his head between her thighs and inhaling her scent. "You smell so good. The aroma of your sweet pussy has been driving me wild." Gripping the top of her panties with both hands, he ripped them off as if the material were tissue paper instead of the sturdy cotton it was actually made of. Then he placed them in his back pocket as he did with her other pair of panties in Atlanta.

"Are you trying to start a collection?"

"The first pair, I keep in a safe place, but these," He patted his back pocket, "I have a plan for. You're not going to get them back, not that they'd provide you with much coverage now, anyway. Do you know what I plan on doing with them?"

Camryn shook her head mutely.

"When I stroke my dick as I think of you, I'm going to hold your cream-smeared panties in my hand until I come. But right now, I'm going to suck your cunt and make you come even harder than I did before." Holding her thighs, he pushed them further apart and did exactly what he'd promised. Eager lips clamped on to her labia, sucking them, creating a delicious pressure that sent fire licking along every single nerve ending in her body. Camryn dug her fingers into his thick, dark hair.

"Oh, Jagger! Lick it!" she cried out, wanton bursts of passion taking over. Common sense had long since flown out into the wind. Right now, all she could think about was how good his mouth felt on her hot sex. If she had to look more closely at what he was doing to her—in the middle of the kitchen and on the table no less—she knew she'd be mortified.

Using his middle finger, Jagger parted her dewy channel and eased his finger into her as far as it could go.

"You're so wet for me, just as I knew you would be." His finger slipped in, then pulled out just to the tip, before it shoved back into her. Her grip tightened in his silky hair. Jagger might not have used his powers to seduce her, but he certainly had a magic tongue. He knew what spots to licks and nip. He was like a maestro and her body was his orchestra. Camryn could no longer deny that this was inevitable like Jagger had stated. She was weak from his slightest touch. The delicious things he did to her were pure sin incarnate. Yet, it wasn't enough. She wanted more.

Jagger's tongue ran along her slit. Camryn's juices already wet her thighs with her need of him. He removed his digit only to replace it with his tongue, thrusting in and out of her, reaching deeper than she suspected most tongues could go. Grinding her pussy against his questing mouth, she rode his face.

Jagger rolled her clit between his thumb and forefinger, creating just enough pressure to send a tingling sensation up her spine. He continued to fuck her with his tongue, showing no mercy.

The boy she'd lost her virginity to, had never come close to making her feel this way. In fact, the entire experience had left her wondering if she was frigid. Now, there was no doubt in her mind that she was not. What had Jagger done to her?

The thought didn't linger long before what felt like an explosion ripped right through her. It slammed her down on the table, her arms too weak to brace her. This didn't make him stop, however. If anything, he focused on her pussy with even more ferocity. He licked and slurped at the gush of wetness her orgasm had produced.

"Jagger, oh, my God! I can't take any more!"

He looked up with a growl. "This cunt belongs to me. Don't stop me while I'm feasting." His eyes were glowing again, and she saw that his fangs were out. Camryn tried to pull away from him, but the grip he had on her thighs kept her immobile.

A prick on her thigh brought her out of her haze. She hadn't expected his bite or that he would feed off her blood but oddly, it wasn't unpleasant. In fact, an exhilarating rush raced from her head to her toes, sending her entire body hurtling to another body-shaking climax.

Her pussy clenched again as though ready for more of his skillful ministrations. When Jagger finally lifted his head, he licked away the blood that stained his teeth and lips. "That was just a sample of what's to come."

He finally relaxed his grip on her, and she used that opportunity to escape, sliding off the table and racing out of the kitchen. She didn't stop running until she made it to her room, where she made sure the door was locked before she crumpled onto the floor in a sobbing heap. She didn't want to feel this way about him, so easily manipulated when he looked at her or touched her. She didn't want to fall in love with him and end up broken because she suspected that if she gave herself to him, he'd own her heart body and soul. She'd be a slave to the passion that only he could induce. She'd completely lose herself. And the scary part was, she knew she was almost there.

She wasn't sure how long she lay there but by the time she stopped crying, her head ached. Camryn wobbled to her feet and dug through her suitcase to find a new part of underwear and a pair of jeans. She'd shower later, when Jagger was otherwise occupied. When she was fully dressed again, she plopped on the bed and closed her eyes to clear her mind. But no sooner did she start to drift off, when a light tap on her bedroom door alerted her to Jagger's presence.

"Go away!"

"Camryn, there is nothing to be ashamed of. We both wanted that. It was inevitable that this happened." Jagger sounded patiently understanding.

"Don't you have the decency to leave me alone? I can't deal with you right now!"

"We'll have to deal with each other eventually. Whether you want to or not, we need to talk. I have something very serious to discuss with you, but I have something else to tell you right now."

"Whatever it is you have to say, I don't want to hear it. You've already demonstrated that you can't be trusted. I told you I didn't want any involvement but you couldn't leave well enough alone."

"Camryn, you weren't exactly protesting. In fact, you had my head gripped so tightly while I was between your lovely thighs, I couldn't have pulled away even if I'd wanted to. Not that I did. Why won't you at the very least admit that you enjoyed it?"

"Just go away, okay? I'm not in the mood to go over the why and how it happened. I'd rather just forget it ever did."

"You know that's not possible, but as I said, we'll leave that conversation for another time because I have something more pressing to tell you."

She pinched the bridge of her nose to ease away the tension headache starting to form behind her eyes. "What?"

"Could you open the door please?"

"Why can't you tell me from where you stand?"

He fell silent.

"Jagger?"

"I just received a call from Uncle Marco."

Camryn jumped off the bed. She practically ripped the door off its hinges when she opened it. Forgotten was any drama between the two of them. "The baby?"

"Yes." Jagger smiled. "Congratulations. You have a little sister."

Chapter Nine

"How are you, kiddo?" Romeo greeted Jagger.

Jagger went into his uncle's embrace relieved to have more people in the house. The arrival of his Uncle Romeo and his family would at least ease some of the tension in the house. Camryn had been avoiding him ever since their lovemaking session. Besides the joy she had expressed at the new arrival of her sister, she hadn't had much to say to Jagger, choosing to hole herself in her room with her cell phone.

"Uncle Romeo, it's good to see you as well, and you, too, Aunt Christine. You look beautiful as always." Jagger walked over to the petite femme standing by Romeo's side, giving her a hug and a kiss on the cheek.

"You're a charmer, just like the rest of the Grimaldi men. How have you been, Jagger?"

"I've been good, but I hear you've been even better. And these two must be Jaxson and Adrienne. They're both as adorable as everyone says they are."

The little girl, whom he knew to be only three, was small for her age. She pulled her thumb out of her mouth to tug on one of her long braids. She stared at Jagger silently as she clung to her father's pant leg. Romeo lifted his daughter into his arms.

"Say hello to your cousin, *piccola*." Adrienne shook her head before burying her face against her father's neck. Romeo stroked the child's hair and shot Jagger an apologetic look. "She's shy, especially around men. Thankfully, she took to me well enough."

"It makes sense. The bond between a parent and a child is a powerful one," Jagger acknowledged.

Romeo kissed Adrienne on the head. "That it is. I knew these two belonged to me the moment I met them. But don't worry about Adrienne, once she warms up to you, she'll be more receptive to you." He turned his attention to the boy beside him. "Jaxson, say hello."

The little boy looked Jagger up and down, intelligent hazel eyes seeming to sum him up. "Hello. Where are you from, mister?" Jaxson finally asked. "You talk funny."

"Jaxson, don't be rude. It's not polite to say things like that," Christine lightly scolded.

"But he does. He sounds like one of the characters from my cartoons. Are you just faking it?" The boy asked.

Christine turned a bright shade of red. "I'd like to apologize for my son in advance. Where our daughter is quiet, our son is very outspoken. He'll say whatever and I mean whatever pops into his mind."

Jagger chuckled. "It's quite alright. There's not enough honestly in the world. Nice to meet you, Jaxson." He held out his hand to the child.

Jaxson eyed his hand suspiciously before giving him a firm handshake. "You still didn't answer my question. Are you faking?"

"Jaxson!" Christine groaned and shot him an apologetic stare.

Jagger chuckled. He liked this kid. "Chto vy dumayete?"

The boy's eyes widened. "That's so cool. What did you just say?"

"I asked, what do you think? That was Russian. Do you know where Russia is?"

Jaxson glared, clearly insulted. "Of course, I do. I have a globe in my room. Will you teach me Russian?"

Jagger nodded. "Of course."

"How about now?" the boy demanded.

"I'm sure you parents would like to get settled in first. But, I promise I will set aside time to teach you. But you must practice even when I'm not giving you lessons. Do we have a deal?"

The boy presented him with a gap-toothed grin. "You got a deal."

"I'm really sorry, Jagger," Christine apologized, although she couldn't quite hide the smile on her face.

Romeo snickered. The older vampire seemed content, his happiness evident. It was quite obvious to Jagger that his Uncle Romeo loved his new family very much. They were a motley crew: an Italian father, Chinese mother, and two African-American children, yet somehow they all fit together. Jagger wanted happiness like that for himself. He vowed he'd have it with Camryn.

As if he'd conjured her up by his thoughts, she came trudging down the stairs with a big smile on her face and wearing a pink sundress, the perfect foil for her dark brown skin. She took his breath away.

"Hi, Romeo."

"How are you, brat?" Romeo greeted back. "I'd hug you, but as you can see, my arms are full. Congratulations on your new little sister. It's quite a feat that your mother actually had the daughter she wanted. Once word gets out, the immortal world will be abuzz. Female-born vampires are rare, and when they reach adulthood, very powerful. I'm sure Marco is strutting around like a peacock."

"Judging from the way he sounded on the phone, he was quite pleased with himself. Very surprised maybe, but extremely happy," Camryn agreed.

"The message that the baby had arrived was on my cell phone when I got off the plane, but I wasn't given any vitals. What is her name?"

Camryn beamed. "Gianna Marie Grimaldi."

Romeo smiled approvingly. "After Mama and Papa."

"They were your parents' names?" Camryn inquired.

"Yes. Forms of them, at least. Mama's name was Maria; Papa, Giovanni."

Jagger frowned. "Isn't that the name of—"

"Yes." Romeo cut him off abruptly. It was clear he didn't want to discuss anything rogue related. Jagger couldn't blame him. The Grimaldi family had suffered at the hands of a rogue hell-bent on destroying them all. Until recently, there hadn't been much cause for celebration but now there was a bounty of good things happening to them; Niccolo had been reunited with his mate and son, Romeo had a new family, and now there was the arrival of a new baby. It was almost like talking about the bad stuff would bring a damper on all the special events.

Christine seemed to notice the sudden tension. "Well, I guess since no one is going to introduce us, I'll have to do it myself. Camryn, right?"

Romeo smiled sheepishly. "I'm sorry, sweetheart, but it is my right as your husband to do the introductions.

Christine, this is the brat, otherwise known as Camryn. Brat, this is the love of my life, Christine."

Camryn offered her hand but Christine pushed it away. "I think we can do better than that. We're family now." Christine pulled Camryn in her arms and the two women hugged.

"And these two angels are my son and daughter, Jaxson and Adrienne. Two of the three reasons I'm happy to wake up each morning."

"Aw, how sweet." Camryn sighed. Her eyes gleamed mischievously. "And I suppose, they're also the reason you no longer go barhopping. Word is, you've been thoroughly tamed."

Romeo grinned at his wife. "I told you she was a brat."

"Pee pee." Adrienne spoke at last.

Christine held out her arms. "I'll take her. Camryn, would you be so kind as to show me where our rooms are?"

"Of course."

Jagger watched Camryn lead Christine and her daughter upstairs.

"Why don't you join your mother and freshen up?" Romeo suggested to his son.

Jaxson looked indignant. "But, I want to hang with the men."

"And you will, son, but you still have pancake syrup on your shirt from this morning's breakfast. Don't you want to change and look your best for when you meet the rest of the family and your new little cousin?"

The child tapped his chin as though trying to weigh his options. "What's in it for me if I do?"

Romeo lifted a brow. "You won't lose your video game privileges."

"Oh. Well, I've given some thought to this matter and I think, it would be a good idea if I do go freshen up." The little boy raced up the stairs.

It was only when Jagger was sure the child was out of earshot that he burst into laughter. Romeo joined him.

"How old is your son?"

"He's six going on forty. He's sharp as a tack, isn't he?"

"He is certainly that."

"Jaxson definitely keeps me and his mother on our toes."

"You sound very proud of him."

Romeo's smile widened. "Extremely. My children had a rough life prior to our adopting them. Their birth mother was a drug addict and they were brought up in an abusive home. Adrienne didn't even speak more than a few words until recently, but Jaxson helps her with new words every day. He's very protective of his sister. And apparently, he already has a little girlfriend in school."

"At six?"

"It's probably mostly kid talk but I can already tell my boy is going to be quite the lady's man when he's older," Romeo bragged. "I have a feeling he'll be beating the girls off with a stick, just like his papa."

Jagger grinned at that. His uncle's conquests were legendary. "And your daughter is precious. She'll have quite a few gentlemen friends of her own."

The smile disappeared from Romeo's face as swift as it had appeared. "The hell she will. Adrienne will never date.

If some punk comes sniffing around my little girl, I'll snap his damn neck."

Jagger could tell his uncle was serious and found the double standard Romeo displayed toward his children very funny because he was sure there would be hell to pay when his daughter was a teenager. He wondered what Christine would have to say about it. "You really love them all, don't you?"

"More than you can ever know. I couldn't love them more if they were from my blood. I used to tease Marco and Nico about them settling down and starting families, but now I know the joy of having one of my own. It is like nothing else, and I wouldn't trade them for all the traveling, barhopping, hell raising, and pussy chasing in the world. I didn't really understand real happiness until Christine came into my life, and adopting the children has been the icing on the proverbial cake."

Jagger had never considered himself an envious man, but he found himself thinking again that he wished to experience the same type of love and relationship with Camryn.

"Why don't you put up your feet? I would imagine your flight must have been exhausting."

"It wasn't that long but it makes a difference when you're traveling with two restless children."

They went into the living room and took a seat on the sofa. Romeo turned to Jagger. "I hope you didn't take offense when I cut you off earlier. I thought it was best if we didn't discuss Underground business in mixed company. Christine is nervous enough with all this *il Diavolo* business and I didn't want her agitated in front of the children."

"That was wise. There's no need to upset them if not necessary," Jagger agreed.

Jagger's eldest uncle, Dante, was the founder and head of an organization they called the Underground, which Jagger had recently joined, that sought to eradicate the rogue threat. Finding *il Diavolo*—and taking him and his minions out—was now the Underground's biggest priority.

"Has Uncle Dante found out who Giovanni is? Is he really your brother?"

Romeo sighed. "It's certainly beginning to look that way to us, and it looks like Adonis may be as well. You know how our kind has a natural feeling of kinship with one who shares our blood?"

"Yes of course. I felt it with my Papa."

"Right. And when we confronted each of these rogues in person, I feel a connection to both. Although naturally, it's not as strong as the bond I have with your father, Marco, and Dante. There are so many unanswered questions that remain."

"Such as?"

"Giovanni called Dante and set up a meeting with him, but he didn't show. Christine won't listen to me, but I think her friend Nya is in league with him; I'm trying to figure out how. Nya came around to our house a couple of weeks ago while I was away. Christine wasn't going to tell me about the visit but I managed to get it out of her. Of course, I wasn't happy about it. I just don't trust her."

"Nya was the tall dark woman with Giovanni?"

"Yes."

"I've seen her before."

"Where?"

"Do you remember when Adonis tricked me into believing he was my father? He took me to one of his homes. She was there."

"What? Why didn't you say anything before?"

"It didn't occur to me to say anything about it until I saw her show up in Scotland with Giovanni. There was so much going on and then I went back to Moscow to do my training with my uncle. I should have said something about it earlier."

Romeo furrowed his brows, his expression serious. "Do you remember anything from the encounter? Anything at all. Did she speak to you? Was she helping him hold you hostage?"

Jagger could tell it was important for Romeo to know about this woman because of his concern for his family but he didn't have much to tell. "We didn't speak. In fact, she didn't acknowledge me. I only saw her the one time and she was heading out. Adonis seemed to be irritated that she was leaving. She seemed...I'm not sure how to describe her. I just remember when I saw her two things ran through my mind."

"What?"

"I remember thinking she was quite stunning and that she didn't seem like she was interested in being around Adonis. It was just a feeling I got from her and I'm not sure why I felt that way."

"Christine mentioned something about her being with someone she isn't happy with. I wonder if she might have been referring to Adonis. Regardless, I can't risk the safety of my family for a hunch. Christine wants to see the good in everyone but she'll just have to accept that not everyone's motives are altruistic."

"You're right. What other things have you worried?"

"We're still trying to figure out who the witch is. All we know is that her name is Liliana and she's connected to Giovanni somehow. Everything is very confusing, especially since that huge confrontation and I'm a bit unsettled with the things going on right now."

"How so? There have been so many good things happening to our family."

"And that's what worries me. There's always been a pattern throughout the years. Whenever something positive happened with the Grimaldi's, something tragic would come along. Things are quiet now and I feel it's giving us a false sense of security. We have to remain on our guard. This is only the calm before the storm. You mark my words, Jagger, the storm *is* coming and it's going to be a big one."

Camryn's heart filled with love when Marc placed baby Gianna in her arms. "She's perfect."

And she was. Camryn ran a finger along Gianna's soft skin, which was a light gold with red undertones. She had chubby cheeks, rosebud lips and a head full of sandy curls. Her ten little fingers and toes were all there and she had that fresh baby powder scent that Camryn loved.

She placed a kiss on the baby's cheek. Gianna responded by opening her eyes and letting out a long yawn. Even her little pink gums were adorable. There were no fangs that Camryn could see which was a plus. Her eyes were still cloudy so the color wasn't evident yet. But Camryn knew her sister would grow up to break many hearts, whether her eyes turned out to be the dark brown of her mother's or the amber shade of her father's.

"Hey, pretty girl, I'm your big sister. It's a good thing you have me to teach you the ropes. You're going to need it in this family.

"Oh, brother. Should I pray for divine intervention now or later?" Marc groaned.

The crowd of family in the room erupted with laugher. Almost everyone was in attendance, including Montana and Oliver, Marc's business partner. Camryn couldn't help but notice the looks those two exchanged every so often. She made a mental note to ask her Aunt Montana about it later because it was clear Oliver was smitten. Even Darren's partner, Bryan, had come to see the baby.

The only one missing was Dante, but Camryn didn't ask too many questions about it because she knew it was a sore subject with her mother and Marc. Besides, she was way too busy getting acquainted with her little sister. Camryn lowered her face to the baby's head, inhaling that wonderful baby smell again. Gianna smiled.

"Do you see this? I think she likes me. This kid has taste."

Her brother, Darren, snorted. "I think it's just gas."

"Shut up, D. You're just jealous because she didn't open her eyes when you held her."

He rolled his eyes and chuckled. "Now, I have two bratty little sisters. Life will certainly get interesting from here on out."

The baby crinkled her little nose and her mouth shaped itself as if to suck. "Uh oh. I think she's hungry." Just as the words left Camryn's mouth, Gianna let out a wail like nothing Camryn had ever heard before. "My sister has a set of lungs on her, too." She reluctantly handed Gianna over to Marc.

"I think you're right." He nuzzled his tiny daughter. "Are you up to feeding her, Maggie?"

Her mother lay against the pillows looking exhausted, but content. "Yes, of course. Give her to me."

When Marc brought the baby to her, the love between the couple was there for everyone to see. It was strong and tangible. "Maggie will need some privacy," Marc announced.

Maggie smiled gratefully, then asked as the room began to clear, "Baby, would it be okay if I had a few words with Camryn alone?"

"Of course, *ciccina*. I'll be in the hallway if you should need me." Marc leaned over the bed and planted a lingering kiss on his wife's lips, and then one on Gianna's cheek. He seemed reluctant to leave mother and daughter.

Once alone with her mother, Camryn averted her eyes as her mother undid the fastening of her gown and offered Gianna a nipple. The baby latched on, sucking hungrily.

Camryn giggled. "She's a greedy little thing, isn't she?"

"Just like her father."

"Gross, Mom. I didn't need to hear that."

Maggie laughed. "Prude."

"I am not. I just don't want to hear about my mother's sex life. It's bad enough that I've heard you and Marc getting it on. On several occasions."

"It's because we love each other." Maggie sighed, stroking the baby's soft curls. "I can't believe she's here and she's everything I'd imagined her to be and more. I feel like I've been pregnant forever. GianMarco and his brothers seem to think having a daughter was an amazing thing, practically a miracle. I think it was meant to be."

"Jagger mentioned it being rare for female vampires to be born. From the way he described it, it happens so rarely that when it does it's a huge deal in the immortal community."

"Well, I always knew. Right from the start."

"So was the labor rough?"

"A little. It has been twenty-two years since I last gave birth, after all, and Gianna weighed nine pounds. I think she probably got that from the Grimaldi side; you and Darren were both just shy of seven pounds." She chuckled. "I think the hardest part was calming GianMarco down. I knew he was worried, but I didn't expect to have a frantic husband hovering over me. It certainly wasn't like my first two go rounds."

"Daddy wasn't in the delivery room with you when we were born?"

Maggie shook her head. "He preferred to stay in the waiting room. I guess some people are just squeamish when it comes to childbirth."

"That's no excuse. Daddy was just being selfish as usual."

"But he was at the hospital each time I delivered. He was so proud of both of you."

"Why do you always defend him? He was a lousy husband and a mediocre father. Do you realize he hasn't spoken to Darren since he came out?"

Maggie frowned. "That's disappointing to hear, but I'm sure he'll eventually regret his decision to not have a relationship with his son."

"I just don't understand how you aren't still angry at how he treated you all those years. You're a saint because I would probably be in jail for committing murder if I were you."

"Camryn, trust me, when your father ended things between us the way he did, I was furious and hurt. And of course, homicide did cross my mind more than a few times, but in order for me to be happy now, I had to let go of the pain and bitterness. Besides, karma is doing a better job than anything I could have ever done to him. Listen, I'm not going to pretend that I had the perfect marriage or that your father isn't without faults but I don't want you or your brother to cut yourselves off from him unless it's something you want to do. Not because of how he treated me."

Her mother probably had the most generous spirit Camryn knew of but it was hard to get past something she'd been holding onto for so long. "I want to let it go to, Mom, I really do but it's hard to move on when every time I talk to him he just uses that opportunity to trash talk about you."

"I'm sorry I can't muster up enough concern to care about what Eugene Williams thinks of me anymore. But at the end of the day, I rarely give him a thought while my name is still in his mouth. If I don't care, you shouldn't either. But let's not talk about him anymore." Maggie shuffled Gianna to her other breast. "I didn't really have the chance to speak to you last night, obviously, so I wanted to do some catching up. How was your trip here? When GianMarco called the house, Jagger told him something about your car giving you trouble."

Camryn groaned as she thought about the junk heap that was her vehicle. "I'll probably have to put a few hundred dollars into it for repairs again, if I'm lucky. More if I'm not."

"Sweetheart, we've offered to buy you a new one. Who knows where you'll be when it breaks down next?"

"Mom, you know I can't let you do that."

"I know how much you value your independence but you're still in school and I don't like the idea of you driving around in that death trap. When I get back home and things have settled down with Gianna, I'm taking you car shopping."

"I'd rather we didn't."

"I insist. Let's just say I'm doing this for selfish reasons. I want you in a road-worthy vehicle and we can more than afford it. Just accept the gift and say thank you."

It wasn't often that her mother took such a firm tone with her so Camryn knew better than to argue. "Thank you."

Her mother smiled. "You're welcome. I know that was hard for you. You've always wanted to do things for yourself and I've admired that about you. By the time you were three, you insisted on picking out your own outfits even though nothing ever matched. And, you liked to make your own lunches for school. I think you even taught yourself how to tie your shoes. It's okay to be self-reliant but there's a difference between independence and foolish pride. I had to learn that lesson the hard way."

Camryn sank back in her chair. She hadn't been expecting a lecture. "Mom, do we have to get into this now?"

"Yes we do, because when I get back home, I'll be surrounded by a houseful of family and I won't have many opportunities to have some alone time with you. My greatest wish as a mother is that my children are happy, but I don't want you to pattern your life based on my mistakes."

Camryn laughed nervously. "I don't know what you're talking about."

"I think you do. Sweetheart, you're not fooling anyone but yourself. What happened between your father and me is in the past. I moved on and found happiness far beyond anything I ever could have imagined. I'm not saying you need a man in your life to make you happy, because of course you don't, but you shouldn't judge all men based on your father."

"Mom, it's easier said than done, especially since I watched you suffer every day. I was there when you shed tears over someone who didn't deserve them. I watched as you were taken for granted and verbally and psychologically abused. I don't want that."

"Who says that'll happen to you?"

"You know I haven't had the best of luck with relationships. Where is all this sudden interest in my love life coming from anyway? Did someone tell you about Jagger?" Camryn could have bit her own tongue out for saying so much.

Maggie smiled knowingly. "No. But you just did. However, I already suspected there was something going on between you because of the way you left so abruptly when you two first met. And then whenever I talked to you on the phone, you mentioned his name a few times. I thought it was odd."

"You didn't press me on it."

"I figured you'd tell me about it when you were ready. You like him, don't you?"

"I don't know."

"Did anything happen in the house while the two of you were alone?"

Camryn lowered her head, unable to look her mother in the eye.

"I'll take your silence as a yes." Her mother transferred the now sleeping baby over her shoulder, adjusted her nightgown, and gently rubbed her back. "Is this just a one off thing or is there more to it? Did he express any feelings toward you?"

"He says that he and I were meant to be—that I'm his mate."

"Oh." Her mother seemed at a loss for words.

"What? You don't approve?" Camryn almost wanted her mother to say no, so she could latch onto any excuse that would prevent her from truly examining her feelings.

Maggie sighed. "It's not that. Can I share something with you?"

"Sure," Camryn answered hesitantly not sure where this conversation was going.

"You're a grown woman and you can do what you want and be with who you want and I'll support you in any decision you make. But there's something you need to know."

194

Camryn released a nervous giggle. "This sounds pretty serious."

"It is actually. It's about Jagger. When a vampire finds his mate, he recognizes her right away. It might not register on a conscious level right away but subconsciously, he knows. Where humans may need weeks, months or even years to decide on something like this, they just know."

"He's only half-vampire, though."

"And he's also half warlock. I don't know much about them but it's my understanding that finding a mate for a warlock is not much different from the vampire way. His warlock half doesn't negate his vampire side. But that aside, the mate thing is a pretty mystical thing amongst immortals, it's not typical for said mate to not return those feeling be that person immortal or human. It's kismet."

"So you're saying I should automatically have feelings for him just because he or some ancient tradition says I should?"

"No. That's not it. But I'm beginning to think that maybe you took off that one time because when you saw him you felt something between the two of you as well."

Camryn shook her head in denial. "No. That's not true."

"Camryn, you're not being honest. I can always tell when you're not telling the truth, you voice gets all high-pitched."

"I can't have feelings for him. It's just not something I planned."

"Love is rarely ever planned. It comes at the most unexpected time and when it does, it can be so beautiful."

Tears stung the backs of her eyes. "Mom, you don't understand. I can't be in love."

"Why not? You could do a lot worse than Jagger. What are you so afraid of?"

"I'm not afraid!" Her raised voice woke Gianna who let out a wail. "Sorry. I've got to go." Camryn stood up with the intention of leaving.

"Sit down," her mother commanded as she stroked the baby's back to calm her down.

Camryn balled her fists at her sides in frustration. She wanted to walk out the door but when Maggie used that tone there was no arguing with her. She plopped back into her seat.

Gianna let out a large belch and promptly went back to sleep. Maggie placed the baby in the basinet on the side of the bed before turning her attention back to Camryn. "What are you afraid of Camryn?" Her mother repeated.

A tear slid down her face. She never realized until this moment how crippling the pain she'd carried with her had been "I'm afraid of losing myself completely to a man and allowing him to take over who I am and what I stand for. I don't like being this way, always looking at every man suspiciously, wondering at his motives. I wish I could be carefree and flirt with men like most of my girlfriends do. Maybe something is wrong with me. When I look back at all my past relationships, I wonder how much of it was me holding my former boyfriends at arm's length. But, I still can't help myself." She planted her face in her palms as the tears fell freely.

Maggie slid to the edge of the bed and got off. She lowered her body to wrap her arms around Camryn. "Baby, it's okay. I know you're scared. I was, too, when I met

GianMarco. Being with an immortal can sometimes be a difficult thing to come to terms with as a human. But, you'll be just fine. You're like me in more ways than you know. You'll love only once, but when you find that love, it'll be forever."

Camryn sniffed. "Are you saying you never loved Daddy?"

"If you would have asked me that over a year ago, I would have said of course I did. But having experienced the real thing, what I felt for your father doesn't compare. To be frank, I loved your father but I wasn't in love with him. What I was in love with was the security I believed he provided and, of course, you and Darren. Growing up, I was in more foster homes than I can count so when your father came along, I truly believed he was my knight in shining armor. But looking back, he was very manipulative from the beginning, making me feel I could never have or do better because of my upbringing. I believed that. Now, I'm very grateful toward him."

"After all he'd done to you?" Camryn asked incredulously.

"Well, if he hadn't left me, I never would have learned how to stand on my own two feet or gain any confidence and because of that, I found something very important."

"True love?"

"That, too, but even more important, I found myself. I learned I don't have to lose a part of who I am again in order to be with the man I love. It can happen for you as well, honey. If you find that special someone who'll treat you like gold, don't be afraid to give him your heart, because he'll nurture and cherish that love, not trample it. Believe me, I have that with GianMarco, and you don't have to look any further than his brothers to see how much they love their women. The Grimaldi men are strong and powerful, but they love deeply, passionately, and possessively."

"And do you think Jagger could be that man?"

Her mother kissed the top of her head. "I think you have to make that decision for yourself."

Camryn sighed. "I know but it's hard."

"These things never are easy but I think you'll make the best decision for you.

Camryn gave her mother a tight hug, glad that they'd had this conversation even though it had gotten off to a bumpy start. She had a lot of food for thought.

"Word of warning: don't toy with his affections. He is a Grimaldi, after all, and they're used to getting what they want."

Chapter Ten

Jagger couldn't think straight. Every time he held Camryn in his arms without properly fucking her, it brought his symptoms back. Each time was more intense than the last. Jagger was fast losing control over his body; the heat would not go away. The chilling spells no longer worked, masturbation only made things worse, and he felt as if he was losing his mind. The ache had become too intense for him to bear.

Something had to be done. He had tried to be patient, to give her space, but it hadn't helped. Ever since she'd gotten back from the hospital, she'd been avoiding him much to his dismay. He'd thought he'd made some headway with her but apparently not. Camryn had even left the house for a couple of days to stay with her brother and Bryan, his lover, only returning when Uncle Marco and Aunt Maggie had brought the baby home from the hospital.

It was frustrating not to be able to have some time alone with her since the entire family was in residence. Everyone had gathered in the living room after dinner but Jagger couldn't concentrate on all the small talk going on around him. His papa and Uncle Romeo were arguing over a chess match, the children were playing some sort of video game, and the women were cooing over the baby while his Uncle Marco played cards with Darren and Bryan. Camryn, however, was nowhere to be found. She'd excused herself, making the excuse of having to work on her thesis. She hadn't come down from her room since.

Frustrated, Jagger headed outside to the patio to clear his head. He gritted his teeth as another wave of heat ripped through his body. It was like someone had doused him with gasoline and threw a lit match at him. He bit down on the inside of his lip so hard he tore into the flesh.

It took more than a few calming breaths to get past this latest attack on his body, but eventually, he cooled down to a more bearable temperature although he remained hot. He plopped down in one of the deck chairs and closed his eyes praying for his pain to end.

"A penny for your thoughts."

Jagger opened his eyes and pasted a smile on his face. He didn't want his father to know the extent of his symptoms. It would ruin the night. "Your chess game is over so soon? The way you and Uncle Romeo were going at it, I imagined the two of you would be playing for hours to come."

Niccolo grinned. "Romeo cheats. Besides, is it a crime that I should want to spend a little time with my son?"

"Not at all. I welcome your company. In fact, it will provide me with a distraction." The entire time he spoke, he kept his gaze averted not wanting his father to guess what was going on with him.

"Jagger, look at me." Niccolo's voice was a soft command.

When he looked in his father's direction, the older vampire recoiled.

"What is it, Papa?"

"Your face and eyes."

Jagger frowned. "What's wrong with my face?" He touched it in a panic. It didn't feel right, misshaped even. "What's happening to me?"

"Don't go anywhere. I'll return shortly." In less than a minute, Niccolo was back with GianMarco and Sasha in tow.

"My baby!" his mother cried in alarm. She rushed to Jagger's side and cradled his head against her breast. "You're burning up! I'll do a cooling spell."

"I've done it already. It doesn't work anymore."

"Perhaps, you should let you mother try. She is a Hectite witch. It can't hurt."

Jagger was unconvinced but anything was worth a try. "Okay, Mama. Do what you must."

Sasha placed her hands on his temples and whispered a chant. The spell only helped a little temperature wise but when he touched his face, if felt normal again.

Sasha looked at her mate. "That spell should have worked. Niccolo, please do something."

Jagger pulled away from his mother and stood up. "There's nothing you can do, Mama. Nothing anyone can do."

"How bad is it, Marco?" his father asked.

"From the look of him, I'm surprised he's been able to maintain enough control not to attack anyone. I vaguely remember what *la morte dolce* was like when I was in the midst of the worst parts of it. Most of the time I could barely think straight, but Dante later told me that when I'd gotten to this point, my mind was no longer my own." Marco studied him closely. "What's probably sustained him so long is his warlock side. *Dio,* I wish Dante were here. He'd know what to do." There was pain in those words. Jagger's heart went out to his uncle, who seemed to be taking Uncle Dante's absence the hardest.

"You spoke to him last, Marco, when did he say he'd arrive?"

Jagger knew everyone wanted to know where his uncle was, but this was the first time the question had been openly asked.

Marco shrugged at Niccolo. "He didn't so your guess is just as good as mine." The tightness in his voice said it all. The topic was no longer up for discussion.

"There's only one way to fix this. GianMarco, can't you speak to Camryn?" Sasha pleaded. "I know it's wrong for me to ask, but look at him. He's in so much pain. I can feel it from where I stand."

"No, Mama. Don't. I don't want her to come to me out of pity. If she does help, it has to be of her own free will."

"But you're suffering!"

"Then I'll suffer. I love her far too much to coerce her. My only option is to leave."

Marco placed his hand on Jagger's shoulder. "You can't go anywhere looking like that. Your eyes are bright red and it won't be long before your face is once again distorted. And it's a pretty good bet that your incisors will lengthen and won't retract."

Jagger laughed without humor at his uncle's words. "Then perhaps people will think I'm wearing a Halloween costume; it is nearly that time, after all. I can't stick around, Uncle Marco. Perhaps, you'll let me borrow one of your vehicles so I can leave tonight."

"Of course, Jagger, but I wish you didn't have to leave this way."

"Why won't you speak to Camryn? This is a family! Aren't we supposed to help each other in our time of need?" Sasha's voice rose to near hysterics.

Niccolo pulled his mate into his arms and rocked her. "Sweetheart, I hurt for our son as well, but Marco is in a precarious situation. His first duty lies with his wife and their immediate family unit, just as you and Jagger are my first priority. This has to be Jagger's decision. I wish he could stay, but having him and Camryn in such close proximity without any love making will only spur him to *la morte dolci* even faster."

"And what will he do when he's in full *la morte dolci?* Are we just going to allow him to suffer needlessly?" The helpless look in his mother's eyes tore at Jagger. He wanted to reassure her that everything would be fine, but he couldn't.

"I'll figure something out, Mama. I could contact Uncle Blade; maybe he'll be able to find a way to contain me once I'm in the midst of this madness. At least he could prevent me from hurting others. Maybe he'll even figure out a way to hold off the symptoms longer until another solution can be found."

Marco shook his head. "Not even the most powerful warlock can hold off *la morte dolci* as demonstrated by your mother. You will suffer no matter what, but as you've just pointed out he might be able to prevent you from harming yourself or anyone else."

"Is it possible I will...I mean, will my mind no longer be my own? Permanently?"

Marco raked his fingers through his hair and exhaled deeply. "It is likely. Listen, I can talk to Camryn, but I'll need to discuss this with her mother first. Just know I won't sway her one way or another when I do have this talk with Carmryn."

"No. I can't have you do that, Uncle. I'll start packing right away and leave once everyone is in bed."

"Are you sure about this Jagger?" Marco asked.

"Yes." Jagger embraced his sobbing mother. "It's okay, Mama. Things will work out, you'll see."

"How will everything be okay when it's possible I'll lose you? When I see you again, you might not recognize who I am. I've lost you once before—I don't think I can bear it again." Sasha wept, wetting his shirt with her tears.

"Mama, please don't cry. You will never lose me here." Jagger pointed to her heart, then he caught a faint movement from the corner of his eyes. Someone had been watching them from inside the house. Could it have been...? No. His imagination was running rampant, which didn't bode well for his future mental state.

Jagger rocked his mother as she clung tightly to him. He met his father's gaze and saw sadness there. Suddenly, he felt like crying himself for what would never be.

<><><><>

The house was finally silent. Camryn tried to gather up the courage she needed to fulfill her plan. "You can do this. It will just be one night." Taking a deep breath, she carefully opened her bedroom door, wincing when it made a loud creak. Closing it behind her, she tiptoed down the hallway to her destination. Not bothering to knock, she twisted the knob and slipped through the door into the dark room. In the shadows, Jagger was haphazardly throwing what appeared to be last-minute items into an overnight bag; he was leaving just as he said he would.

His head shot up. She nearly lost her nerve when she found herself staring into glowing eyes. She couldn't make out his features but thought he was probably surprised to see her in his bedroom.

"What are you doing here?" he growled. Jagger's voice sounded deeper, gruffer, and more guttural. She could hear the pain in his words and tone.

Camryn wasn't sure what kind of reception she'd been expecting but it wasn't this exactly. She nearly lost her nerve. "I think you know why I came."

"Do I? Look, Camryn, it's not safe for you to be here and, frankly, I'm not in the mood for games."

"Who said I'm playing games? I want to help you."

"So it was you earlier. How much did you hear? Or did Uncle Marco have that talk with you after all?"

"No. Actually, he didn't get a chance to talk to me. You told him not to remember? I heard what you said outside. I didn't mean to eavesdrop, but when I passed the patio door, it was slightly open. When my name was mentioned I couldn't help but listen to your conversation."

"So you're graciously offering your body to me after avoiding me like the plague?"

A lump that felt like the size of a golf ball formed in her throat. She wasn't sure how she could explain what she'd been going through these past few days. It was true that she'd been purposely avoiding him but it was mainly to come to terms with her feelings for him.

When she wasn't avoiding him, she had a chance to observe the kind of man Jagger was. He played with the children, giving them piggyback rides, and seemed genuinely interested in what they had to say. He was affectionate with his parents. It was apparent that he cared about all his family. He had a sense of humor that made her giggle and often caught her off guard. And he had often brought a smile to her face in spite of herself. She wanted to tell him about the conversation she'd had with her mother at the hospital and why she'd fought so hard against the attraction she felt from him day one. But that would have to come later.

For now, there was a more pressing issue. Jagger was ill. She didn't know what *la morte dolci* was but what she'd gotten out of the conversation was that he was in a lot of pain and only she could help. She didn't want him to suffer especially when she wanted to be with him as badly as he wanted to be with her. Already, her body trembled with anticipation as she thought of his lips and tongue roaming every inch of her. She wanted to feel the intoxicating sensations she'd only ever experienced in his arms. Camryn desperately wanted his hands and mouth all over her.

Each night, she'd lain awake with carnal thoughts of the two of them. The images of his thick cock sliding deep inside her pussy were enough to keep her panties damp and her knees weak. When she'd listened to how much he'd suffered because she'd stayed away, she realized she was fighting a losing battle where he was concerned. She wanted Jagger Grimaldi, too, and by the end of the night, she vowed, she'd have him. And he could have her, any way he liked.

The very idea that she could drive him to near insanity frightened her a little but she trusted that he wouldn't hurt her. Hearing that he was willing to sacrifice his sanity because he didn't want to force her into something she didn't want, helped her make her decision about him. Jagger was an honorable man and helping him in his moment of need was the least she could do.

"Yes," she finally answered.

He remained silent. The only sound in the room was his ragged breathing, deep and shallow. Jagger turned his back to her and resumed packing.

"Jagger?" She felt uncertain; she'd been so sure he'd jump at her offer, but she hadn't expected rejection.

"While I appreciate your willingness to surrender your delectable body, I'll have to decline."

"What?"

"I don't want or desire a little girl in my bed who thinks she's doing me a favor by coming to me. I need a willing woman who wants to be here."

Her face warmed from her embarrassment. If Camryn didn't think he was worth it, she would have left him alone. But she couldn't walk away. Not like this. "I *am* here because I want to be."

"After ignoring me these past few days?"

"I had a lot of thinking to do and I couldn't do that with you around. I'm sorry, but I had to be sure about us."

"Us? Since when has there ever been an 'us'? You've made it quite clear you're not interested in anything long term. Or maybe you just enjoy having your pussy licked. Well, Camryn, if you stay in this room, I'm going to do more than perform cunnilingus on you. Much more. So are you ready to be thoroughly fucked?"

Camryn gulped. She wasn't sure if she liked this uber aggressive Jagger but it had to be because of his condition. She took a deep breath, determined to not run away. "If-if that's what you want."

"Oh, you have no idea what I want. The question is, are you willing to give it to me?" Before she could respond, Jagger stood in front of her as if he'd teleported across the room. She took a step away from him, but Jagger followed until her back touched the door.

Camryn tried not to tremble when his hand spanned her throat, his thumb grazing her pulse. "I'm here, aren't I?"

"Yes, you are, indeed. But you never answered my question. Will you let me do whatever I want to you?"

Camryn nodded, her voice caught in her throat, her heart pounding rapidly.

"Will you let me finger your clit while my tongue slides in and out of your cunt? What about if my tongue glides along the crack of that luscious ass of yours, tasting you there?"

She licked her lips. "Well, it's nothing you haven't already done to me, so yes." Just thinking about him doing it to her again sent a lightning bolt of anticipation up her spine.

"Will you let me fuck you until you can barely move even after I've made you come over and over again?"

"Yes," she whispered, her heart speeding up with each sinful image that popped into her head.

"What about letting me fuck your mouth? I can see it now, me sliding my cock between your soft lips while I dig my fingers in your hair. Your lips would be wrapped around my dick nearly as tight as your pussy. I saw the way you looked at my body, and I know you want to taste me, too."

"I do. Oh, God, I do." Camryn turned her head away, unable to meet those glowing eyes almost ashamed that she was so turned on by his frank language.

"And your ass? Will you let me fuck it, too? Because if you stay, I will. I want to be inside all your holes, with my fingers, my mouth, and my cock—all over you."

Camryn knew he was trying to run her off but she refused. She could be quite stubborn if she wanted to. Besides, how could she walk away when her panties were wet, her breasts tight, and her body on fire?" "You're not going to scare me into leaving, Jagger."

With a snap of his fingers, the lights turned on. She bit down on her bottom lip to stop the scream forming in her throat from escaping.

"How about now, Camryn? Do you still want me now when I look like this?" Jagger's eyes were completely red. He looked like he was wearing novelty contact lenses. His pupils were no longer visible. His eyebrows were raised in an almost caricature-like distortion, and his fangs were out and menacing. All this, coupled with his flared nostrils, reminded her of the very monster she'd been afraid of, but instead of fleeing, compassion filled her heart.

What he must have suffered and undergone touched her deeply. With a trembling hand, she reached out and caressed the side of his face. This was obviously not the reaction he'd expected given the baffled expression in his eyes.

"Why aren't you running away?"

"Because I did this to you and you're in pain. And because I want to make it better. Please let me." Standing on the tip of her toes, she kissed him where his neck and shoulder met. The contact nearly burned her lips, but she didn't pull away. With trembling fingers, she started to unbutton his shirt.

"Camryn," he growled. "This is your final warning. If you stay, I'm going to take you, and I won't be gentle."

"It's okay. I'm yours, however you want me." She opened his shirt to reveal the hair-roughened expanse of his chest, then pressed a kiss against the flat disk of his nipple.

"Camryn."

She could tell he was struggling to hold onto his control, but she didn't want him to. Jagger clenched and unclenched his fists. "Why suffer when you don't need to?" she whispered, then circled the now-taut peak with her tongue, his musky male flavor adding a tinge of piquancy to her taste buds.

"I don't want your pity, Camryn."

"Does this feel like pity?" Boldly, she cupped her hand between his legs, giving the bulge she found there a light squeeze. With a barely surprised roar, Jagger grabbed her hand, yanking it from his body before he lifted her and strode the short distance to the bed. He dropped her in the center none too gently.

"You're damned right you've driven me to this, Camryn, and you're going to get what you've been denying both of us." With each word, he tore at his clothing, exposing his chiseled body to her hungry gaze. "You'd better take off your clothes or they'll be nothing but confetti once I get my hands on them."

His warning sent her into action. Hurriedly, she pulled the nightshirt over her head. Camryn felt another blush sweep her cheeks when she revealed her nakedness to him. Jagger looked slightly disappointed. "No panties? Pity. I was looking forward to adding another pair to my collection."

Camryn suddenly felt self-conscious about her body even though he'd already seen most of her. She crossed her arms over her breasts.

"Drop your hands, *milaya moya*. Perfection such as these should not be hidden in my presence." She did as he said. "There's no need to be ashamed of these beautiful breasts. They're perfect with big suckable nipples. And your skin is so soft. I've thought of nothing else but touching you all over. Don't ever cover yourself like this again." He stared at her with such blatant lust, her breath caught in her throat.

Camryn didn't have a chance to say anything else before he sprang onto the bed, covering her body with his. Jagger was hot, more so than any living thing should have been. Instead of kissing her mouth as she thought he would, he placed frantic kisses over her face and neck, then slid down her body.

She gasped when his incisors grazed her throat, breaking the skin, but that didn't stop the delectable sensations forming throughout her body. His hands were everywhere, her breasts, stomach, thighs, and pussy. Camryn squirmed beneath him, eager for more than just kisses. She'd come to his room with every intention of offering the relief he needed, but she wanted this just as much as he did. Camryn couldn't believe she had fooled herself into believing she could stay away from him.

"Jagger, please," she begged, not quite sure what she was asking for.

He spread her legs roughly; he'd told her he would, but it still surprised her. But this was not her gentle-but-insistent vampire. This Jagger was hungry—and the only sustenance he appeared to want was her.

He dug his fingers into her thighs as he rested his head between them. "Ah, I'll take that little girl comment back. This is most definitely a woman's cunt, so wet and ready to be licked, sucked, and fucked. And it's ready for my mouth and cock. Don't ever shave it." Lowering his head, he parted her labia with his tongue before clamping down on her clit.

"Oh, Jagger," she cried out before realizing how loud she'd been. She bit her lower lip, not wanting to wake the rest of the house. He suckled on the throbbing bundle of nerves, making her writhe uncontrollably beneath him. She gripped his shoulders, her nails biting into his hot flesh. When Jagger slid a finger into her, Camryn thought she'd go insane.

Bucking her hips, she ground against him, unable to handle the torturous bliss of his mouth. Jagger continued to suckle, unheeding of her movements, slipping yet another finger into her slick channel. He twisted and thrust his digits into her with skilled precision.

"Jagger." She moaned his name as loudly as she dared.

He lifted his head then, eyes still blood red. "Don't be afraid to call out my name."

"But the others..."

"Uncle Marco has recently soundproofed the bedrooms, so what we're doing can't be heard by human ears. But what do you think is going on in nearly every bedroom right now, Camryn? At this very moment, my mama and papa are calling out each other's names in their passion for each other. Uncle Romeo and Christine are doing the same. Even your mother and Uncle Marco—"

"Stop. Don't say any more."

"It is the truth. We are a passionate lot. Give over to your desire for me. Scream my name as loudly as you want." Lowering his face between her legs again, he lapped at her pussy with long, broad strokes, the actions sending torrents of pleasure throughout her sensitized body.

"Jagger!" she shrieked. "Oh, God, Jagger!"

Chapter Eleven

The more he tasted of her, the more Jagger wanted. No matter what he did, he couldn't get enough of Camryn. The sweet cream of her cunt flowed freely, and he drank every bit that escaped from her wet channel. He had to be inside of her now, but Jagger had just enough sanity left to know that if he took her as he wanted, he'd hurt her.

Gliding up the length of her body, his mouth covered hers. She met the thrust of his tongue, hers joining his in a sensual dance as old as time. The blood lust within Jagger drove him to gently nip her tongue. She gasped, trying to pull it back, but his strong lips captured it, and he drew it further into his mouth.

Jagger wanted more of her blood. Releasing her tongue, he caught her lower lip.

"Jagger, what are you doing to me?"

He couldn't stop himself even if he wanted to. He bit and sucked, then licked. Unable to hold off any longer, he rolled onto his back, bringing Camryn on top of him. "Straddle me, *milaya moya.*"

She hesitated for only a moment, and then did as she was told.

"You're going to ride my cock, and while my staff is inside your cunt, I want you to lean over while I feast on your nipples."

Camryn shivered in reaction to his words; her lust-glazed eyes proved she wanted this as much as he did. She looked so beautiful hovering over him, her lips swollen from his kisses. Jagger was afraid he'd wake and this would all just be a dream.

"Take my cock in your hand."

She ran her tongue over his lips and wrapped slender fingers around his erection. The contact on his engorged flesh sent electric charges surging through him. He caught her by the waist, lifting her until her pussy was positioned over the helmet of his cock.

"Spread yourself for me with your other hand; open your cunt for my cock."

She looked uncertain for a moment. "You're so big. I don't know if I..."

"You will take every inch of me. You are my woman, and you'll get used to my size, because I plan on partaking of your sweet pussy and tight ass as often as possible. Now, part yourself. This is what you wanted to do. Your cunt is already wet and ready for me."

Camryn spread her labia. Only then did he lower her, congratulating himself on his rigid control. When his cock head made it inside her channel, it took everything in him not to spear right into her.

"Oh, God! It's-I've never been stretched like this before."

"Relax. Just let go, and feel me." He lowered her further, gritting his teeth with pleasure. Goddamn, she was incredibly tight.

Camryn wiggled as if trying to adjust herself to him, and that was Jagger's undoing. He brought her down fully on his dick.

She let out an agonized scream. "Oh my God!" She tried to move, but he held her firmly against him. Her pussy fit around him like a wet velvet glove.

"Take it easy. It will get better." He groaned at the exquisite agony, knowing he couldn't move or he'd cause her further discomfort.

She closed her eyes with gritted teeth. "It's a little uncomfortable. You're so frigging big."

"Relax, *milaya moya*. Your body is tense. Let it accustom itself to my cock. Yes...that's it. I promise I won't move until you tell me otherwise, but please don't make me wait too long. I burn for you, ache for you."

She looked unsure.

"Trust me." He grazed her clit with the pad of his thumb, lightly at first and then he started to stroke it. Camryn inhaled sharply as his finger slid along her slit.

"Do you like this?"

She nodded.

"Good, because I like doing it to you. I love the way you're so tight and slick for me. Your pussy took every inch of my dick, didn't it?"

"Yes, but I didn't think it would." Her whisper was breathy.

"Yet it did. You should have believed me when I said your body was made exclusively for mine." He stroked her throbbing clit with each word. "I've never seen such a tempting sight as your lovely dark body, so perfect in form just waiting for my kisses and caresses."

Camryn placed her hand against his chest, trembling violently. He knew she was turned on again. The very heat emanating from her pussy was enough to set them both on fire.

"Tell me how much you want this."

"I do."

"Say the words!" he roared, squeezing her clitoris with enough pressure to make her gasp, but not enough to cause pain.

"I want you. Please take me now. I need you, Jagger!"

"Tell me how much you want to be fucked. Tell me you love my cock in your pussy."

"Fuck me, Jagger! Do it now! I don't think I can stand it any longer; I need you." She groaned almost as if she were the one in agony. He smiled then, knowing how sinister and smug he must appear. She turned her head away, looking slightly ashamed.

"Look at me, *milaya moya*." Camryn faced him until their eyes met once again. "We are doing nothing wrong. This is something we both want. Let me show you how good it can be between us."

Holding her by the waist once more, Jagger raised her, her pussy sliding along his hardened shaft, causing them both to moan at the titillating sensation. Then he lifted his hips and thrust deeply into her, holding her still as he moved. This gave him a chance to study the expressions on her face. Her lips were slightly parted now and her eyes gleamed with passion.

She dug her fingernails into his chest, her breast jiggling back and forth with each thrust. "Oh, Jagger, this feels so good. I never thought I could be filled like this. I doubt any other man will ever measure up to you."

At the mention of other men, a feral need to show Camryn just who she belonged to took over. "There will be no other men after me!" And to underscore his point, he drove deeper, harder, and faster into her tight hole, branding her his. Camryn's cries of wanton abandonment greeted his ears.

His!

Camryn was all his!

She belonged only to him!

Jagger shifted positions, sitting up so that they could now face each other. She wrapped her legs around his waist at his command. His hunger for her drove Jagger to the brink of madness. Leaning forward, he captured a hard nipple in his mouth, sucking and nibbling on it, savoring the heady flavor of her skin.

"Jagger!" She screamed, clawing at his back. "I'm going to come!"

Releasing the taut tip with a pop, he pumped harder than ever, his own peak near. "Don't hold back. Don't ever hold anything back from me." Her breast looked far too tempting to not taste. He sank his teeth on the side of the plump flesh. Camryn buried her face into his neck, her fingers digging into his skin, and her pussy muscles clenching tighter around his member. His orgasm came with an earth-shattering jolt.

Camryn reached her climax almost simultaneously, her body shaking and more delicious cream spilling from between her thighs. The coppery sweet flow of her blood in his mouth heightened the sensation of their climaxes. Lifting his mouth, Jagger felt his incisors retract and the heat he'd been suffering was abruptly gone. But his need for her had not lessened.

Lying on his back again, Jagger lifted Camryn off his cum-soaked shaft and pulled her up the length of his body until her cunt rested just over his lips, their mingling juices dribbling from her pussy.

"Jagger no! We just—"

"Just fucked? Do you think the taste of you and me mixed so lovingly together disgusts me? No, *milaya moya*, this is one way my kind feeds and I'm going to do it now, just like this."

Camryn covered her face. "But it..." Her words trailed off when he brought her pussy down on his mouth. Their mingled juices excited him. Loving her this way had been a fantasy of his since he'd first seen her. He shot his tongue inside her channel. Camryn wiggled and squirmed, groaning.

"Jagger, you're driving me crazy." He knew it was true; her body told him so. Never had he been with someone so responsive to him. Jagger sucked and licked her until she writhed like a wild woman. He didn't stop until the warm gush of her desire filled his mouth again.

He drank her essence, making him stronger than ever before. Camryn moaned and sighed, arching her back and offering even more of herself to him. Only when he had taken what he needed, did he move her off his face and lay her on the bed.

Camryn looked at him her eyes filled with wonder and an emotion he couldn't quite make out, although he hoped it was the one he wanted it to be. She touched his cheek. "Your face is back to normal," she whispered.

"You've helped me through the worst of my suffering, but don't think I'll let you get away so easily from me."

"I didn't know it could be like this. I mean, I knew it would be good, but I couldn't have expected it to be this earth shattering."

Jagger stroked the damp hair plastered to her forehead. "That should tell you we are meant to be together. Get some rest, *milaya moya*, because you're going to need it."

Camryn was having the most delicious dream. She lay on the beach under the warmth of the sun, her body naked beneath its heated rays. Butterflies flitted across her face, tickling her skin, still slightly damp from a swim in the ocean. Her pussy tingled. Something nudged her thighs apart and heat invaded her body.

She opened her eyes to discover she hadn't been dreaming at all. The warmth she'd felt was Jagger's body on top of her, moving deep inside of her. She sighed at the decadent sensations surging through her. A lazy smile tugged the corners of her lips as she wrapped her arms around his neck, her hips lifting to meet his thrusts.

"Mmm, what an interesting way to wake up."

"I thought you'd never open your eyes. You sleep like the dead. I've been playing with your gorgeous body for what seems like hours."

"It couldn't have been that long. It's still dark out."

"Okay, maybe a few minutes, but every second without you is an eternity to me."

Camryn felt a twinge in her heart. No one had ever said anything so touching to her before. With each passing second she spent with Jagger, she knew she'd made the right decision to come to him. She still didn't think this was the time to have the talk they needed to have about their future. She wanted to make sure he was completely out of the woods as far as his sickness went. Camryn wanted him to have a clear mind while she expressed her concerns and fears.

She hoped she wasn't wrong in thinking they could have something special together. She clung to him, staring into his eyes. His gaze was like a gentle caress.

"You're so beautiful," he whispered.

"Oh yeah? I must be because you keep telling me that," she teased.

"Look no further than a mirror and you'll see the truth." He closed his eyes and growled. "Your pussy is so tight. I'll never get enough of it."

"I'll never get enough of you either."

He opened his eyes to stare at her again. "Don't say things you don't mean woman."

"I do mean it."

His cock pulsed within her now, the hard wall of his chest crushing her breasts. No more words were needed as they ground, slid, and moved together. Camryn's arms tightened around him when they both climbed the heights of ecstasy to their mutual satisfaction. Their mouths melded together; the kiss was hot, hungry and needy. She could still taste the two of them on his tongue.

Camryn pressed closer to him. She wanted this man so much she didn't know how to handle it. When Jagger finally lifted his head, Camryn could hardly catch her breath.

"Camryn, I need you again."

She giggled. "Already? You want more? You're insatiable."

"You had to know that a few times would not be enough. Remember when I said I wanted your ass?"

She shuddered. "I...If that's what you want. I've never done it before, but I'll trust that you'll be gentle with me."

Amber eyes twinkled with amusement. "Weren't you the one who promised I could have you any way I wanted? You are many things, *milaya moya*, but I never thought a coward was one of them. Who would have thought a little ass play would frighten you so."

"Coward! Me? I am not a coward. Wouldn't any woman be nervous at the threat of your humongous penis?"

"My size is not so great."

Was he kidding? "According to whom? The Jolly Green Giant? That thing should have its own ZIP code."

Jagger chuckled. "You had no problem riding it earlier."

"After a lot of adjusting."

"What happened to my brave little spitfire? Are you going to go back on your word?"

"I didn't say that, either."

"Prove it."

She'd never been one to turn down a challenge. Camryn's eyes narrowed slightly with determination. "How do you want me?"

"On your hands and knees." Jagger rolled away from her, giving her the opportunity to move into the position he wanted her. He shifted behind her, grasping her hips, and she trembled with fear, thinking she must be crazy to go through with this. Never in a million years would Camryn have thought she'd be having anal sex, but she wasn't foolish enough to believe curiosity didn't play a part in this. He'd made her feel good in so many other ways, why not this one?

"Camryn, for this to be an enjoyable experience for you, you'll need to completely relax," he commanded with a soft whisper.

She took deep breaths, trying to do exactly that. "Don't you need...I mean, you will use lube, won't you?"

"Yes, only the best kind." He reached between her legs and eased two fingers inside her pussy. Camryn quivered as an instant surge of passion sped through her. Jagger slid those digits in and out of her several strokes, then pulled them out.

Her gently spread her cheeks and rubbed those dew-slicked fingers across her puckered hole. Camryn resisted the urge to flinch, or at the very least clench her buttocks tight. Jagger soothed her, whispering in Russian. His ministrations began to elicit the heat she'd felt earlier.

She cried out when his fingers slipped past her tight ring.

"Easy, my love. Easy."

"I'm not sure if I like this," she said honestly when he was knuckle deep.

"Give it a chance; it's all I ask."

Camryn relaxed as best as she could, allowing him to finger her ass. Jagger took things slow. At last, she began to feel the old familiar stirrings of lust. He must have hit a certain spot, because she shuddered with delight.

"That's it, my love," he crooned encouragingly.

She soon found herself pushing against his steadily moving digits.

Jagger leaned over and kissed the nape of her neck. "Do you like this?"

"Yes."

"Are you ready for my cock?"

"Mmm, as ready as I'm going to get."

"When I enter you, push."

"Push?"

"It sounds strange but it will make it easier, I promise."

She bit her lip, preparing herself for his invasion. Jagger removed his fingers and replaced it with the tip of his dick. "Oh, my God!" she squeaked, more from surprise than pain. She gnawed the inside of her mouth when his massive cock gradually slid into her. He stilled, and she knew it was for her benefit. She appreciated his thoughtfulness. It took few moments before the discomfort vanished. Camryn shifted against him, taking more of his length.

Jagger groaned, grasping her hips. "Don't move unless you mean it."

"I do." By now, waves of carnal gratification like electric currents dipped through her entire being. He pushed balls deep into her ass. Camryn yielded to him completely, aroused by the newness of these sensations. Ecstasy licked her nerve endings.

"So round and big; this ass was made for fucking." His palm slapped one tender butt cheek.

"Oh!" She certainly hadn't expected that. "You're asking for trouble, buddy."

"Is it not my right to do what I wish with this ass?"

She squealed, not sure if she should be upset or laugh at him. "Your ass?"

"Yes, mine."

"Just as I suppose your cock belongs to me?"

"Of course. We belong to each other. God, you're so incredibly delicious. I'm so close to coming I don't know if I can hold on."

Camryn's fingers clutched the sheets, her arms holding her braced as Jagger pounded into her, his balls slapping against the seat of her ass. He pumped harder, creating an erotic hurt like nothing she'd thought she could possibly enjoy, but she did. She loved it, loved the feel of his cock in her ass.

Jagger reached around and rubbed her clit, intensifying the already explosive yearning within, and then howled his climax moments later, his seed shooting into her tight bottom. When her orgasm hit soon after, Camryn collapsed, unable to endure such feverish sensations any longer. Jagger followed her down, sliding his dick from her rear and pulling Camryn into his arms. He kissed her shoulder.

"Now that wasn't so bad was it, *milaya moya*?"

Camryn had to admit it hadn't been. "It was much more pleasant than I expected."

"I promise I'll make it even better the next time."

"You sound very confident that there will be a next time?"

"Oh, I know there'll be."

"How are you feeling?"

"Better than I have for weeks. I feel like I can breathe again."

She raised her head to look him in the face. "You were in a lot of pain, weren't you?"

"More than you can imagine."

"I'm sorry."

"For what?"

"For making you wait and for putting you through that horrible ordeal."

"You couldn't have known. Don't beat yourself up over it."

"Jagger, I meant what I said earlier about not being here out of pity. I wanted this as much as you did and I've been silly for fighting it."

Jagger kissed the top of her head. "You weren't silly. I'm sure you had your reasons and we'll have more time to discuss them later but for now, let's go take a shower. The warm water should relax your muscles some."

Camryn felt a blush creep over her skin. She was a bit sore. "Good idea. We have to make sure no one is in the hallway."

"I think we'll be okay. As I said earlier, everyone is either sleeping or otherwise preoccupied, like we'll be soon enough."

Camryn grinned. "Why do I get the feeling you have more than just a shower in mind?"

"Because I do. You know me so well, *Milaya moya.*"

Camryn realized she'd have no chance of getting any sleep for the rest of the night and probably the next day if Jagger had any say in the matter. And she didn't mind one bit.

Chapter Twelve

Adonis pushed deeper into Nya's snug cunt. He could fuck her a million times, but it would never be enough. His need for her consumed him when she wasn't around. She had been an obsession for him from the moment he'd laid eyes on her. Her dark skin against the paleness of his created a sensual contrast he found utterly erotic. But she was a quiet lover, gasping and moaning softly. He knew she pretended not to want him, but her wet pussy told him otherwise. One day he'd have her screams.

He shot his seed into her slick channel, filling it before falling on top of her. He captured her plump bottom lip between his teeth, nibbling none too gently. When Nya attempted to turned her head away, he caught her chin and held it firmly.

"Don't look away from me, my beauty. You've denied me your presence for too long. You have been very naughty lately, haven't you?"

She averted her gaze, lips firming into one thin line. He hated when she wouldn't give her all to him. Her secrets drove him insane, and he hated that he couldn't get inside her head. In most circumstances he could, but Nya was the mistress of keeping herself closed off to people, especially to him.

"Look at me, Nya," he commanded gruffly.

With apparent reluctance, she finally met his gaze, her expression unreadable.

"I wonder what you hide behind those lovely brown eyes."

"You have my body. I come when you call. That should be enough. My thoughts belong to me."

"But that's where you're wrong. I own you; heart, body, and soul."

Her eyes glowed. "No one can ever own me! Never again! Get off of me."

Adonis chuckled in the face of her rage. He preferred her anger to her mock indifference, it demonstrated the passion he so admired within her. "Perhaps it doesn't suit me to do so." He leaned over and ran his lips against her throat.

"So beautiful." He allowed his incisors to descend and sunk them into her tender flesh without warning.

Nya cried out as he fed from her. There was no taste quiet like hers and he'd had many. It was only when she pushed against his shoulders and whispered, "enough," did he stop.

She stared at the ceiling, her eyes slightly glazed. "Please, get off," Nya said softly.

He smirked. "Since you asked nicely." He rolled off, licking his lips and savoring the taste of her on his tongue.

Nya didn't move. He contemplated pulling her into his arms but thought better of it. She could be unpredictable in moments like this. Besides, there were more pressing matters. He needed information. "You've been away longer than expected. Where did you go?" He knew very well where she'd been, but for once he wanted to hear it from her lips.

"I...I had something I needed to take care of."

"What?" he demanded again, losing his patience with her secretiveness.

"Nothing important."

"That nothing important being your friend, Christine Grimaldi?"

Her eyes widened. Adonis smiled with satisfaction. Other than in bed, it wasn't often he could wring a reaction from her. "You didn't think I knew, did you? You may be able to allude the guards I have watching you sometimes, but I have other means of learning your whereabouts. I'm getting tired of your disappearing and coming and going as you please."

"Leave Christine out of this. Your vendetta doesn't lie with her." Nya actually sounded concerned. His heartless femme actually did have feelings it seemed. How touching.

He rolled on top of her, cupping her face in his palms. "My vendetta, as you so quaintly put it, is with the entire Grimaldi family. Hasn't she just recently mated with Romeo? The very one who foiled my plan with the Council? I plan to pay my little brother back for that one. And it's my understanding, they have two children. What are their names? Oh yes, Jaxson and Adrienne. It would be ashamed if something happened to such innocents." He laughed, taunting her with his knowledge.

Nya wiggled from beneath him—only because he allowed it. "Don't you dare harm them!"

"And what do you propose to do about it? Who's going to stop me? Certainly not you, my beautiful traitor."

Nya hopped off the bed and grabbed her clothes, hurriedly throwing them on.

"Don't think warning her will do you any good, because there's nothing that can stop what's about to happen to them."

She paused in the midst of zipping up her black leather pants. Her tight black T-shirt, two sizes too small, emphasized her braless breasts and showed off her flat stomach. His cock rose once again. He was tempted to pull her back on the bed and fuck her senseless, but decided he'd have plenty of time later.

"What are you planning to do?"

"Why do you want to know, Nya? So you can run and tell my brother of my plans? I think not. You think you're safe with Giovanni, but I'm always one step ahead of him and my younger brothers. Watch your step, Nya. My desire for you won't prevent the repercussions you'll suffer if you continue to defy me by going to him. The freedom you think you have is only what I've granted you. Make no mistake about it: I made you, and I can just as easily destroy you."

"You are twisted."

"I am what *they've* turned me into, but I, at least, know which side I'm on. Whose side are you on?"

She glared at him briefly and, for a second, he almost felt hate emanating from her. Adonis shook his head with a smile. She could hate him all she wanted, but Nya would soon realize his true power.

"Mine," she said simply. She turned to leave.

"Where are you going?" he demanded harshly.

"Out."

"When will you be back?"

"Maybe I won't be."

"Oh, you'll be back, or I'll track you down and drag you back. Don't stay away so long this time…and give my regards to Robyn."

She halted in mid-step, but didn't turn to face him.

"Ah, your other little secret," he taunted. "Take care, Nya."

She trembled and her fists clenched at her sides. For a second, he thought she'd turn around and rage at him. Instead, she squared her shoulders and stormed out the door, slamming it behind her. Adonis chuckled to himself. There was so much fire in her. In the nearly two hundred years since he'd found her, Nya had never bored him like many women had in his lifetime. It was one of the reasons he allowed her so much leeway, but there was only so far he'd let her go.

Nya probably believed she was the one in control, but she'd soon fall in line. A smile touched his lips. She likely wouldn't heed his warning about the younger Grimaldis and would try to warn Giovanni, but it wouldn't do any good. He chuckled. She could warn them all she pleased because it suited him for her to do so. That way, when his plan was completely implemented, they'd wonder what the hell had happened. He'd waited too long for the perfect revenge, but now the time had come.

He'd ruin all their love, and just when they wished they'd never been born, he'd destroy them. Each and every one of them.

Adonis laughed as he picked up his phone and called one of his contacts. "Ulm, she's left the house. Follow her and don't let her out of your sight unless you want to meet your death—I promise it won't be swift or merciful." He hung up.

It was time.

Jagger rested his head on Camryn's lap as she absently stroked his hair. He hadn't felt this content for a very long time. Being with Camryn like this made everything he'd gone through worth it. After they'd made love several times, he had feared she'd go back to avoiding him but was pleasantly surprised when she didn't. In fact, she was not only receptive when he made advances toward her, she initiated contact plenty of times herself.

The two of them had volunteered to take Jaxson and Adrienne to the park for a picnic lunch. They had eaten and were now watching the children play. Everything seemed perfect but Jagger could tell something was on her mind; she'd been silent for most of the day.

"What's wrong, sweetheart?"

"Nothing's wrong but everyone knows what's happened between us."

"And you enjoyed every minute of what happened."

"Of course I did. It was just embarrassing when everyone was teasing us. Mom wouldn't stop looking at me with that smug grin, I caught Marc snickering a couple times and Romeo has been absolutely merciless. He keeps saying I'm walking funny. I wanted the floor to swallow me when he said that. And you mother, called me daughter. It was just a bit overwhelming."

"They mean no harm and there's absolutely nothing to be ashamed of Camryn. What we did was natural. No one thinks badly of us. You are my bloodmate. We would have eventually made love even without *la morte dolci*."

"But under my mother's roof? If anyone had told me that I'd do that, I would have called them a liar. All the noise we made could have awakened the dead, soundproofing or no soundproofing."

"You have to remember that most of us aren't human. We don't live by human rules, remember that. No one is judging you, I promise."

Jagger turned his head to see what the children were up to. Jaxson was pushing his little sister on the swings. Adrienne screamed with glee, pumping her little legs and trying to go higher.

Jagger smiled at the scene. "Aren't those two adorable?"

"Yes. They're good kids. It will be interesting to see what it's like for them growing up with Romeo as a father." Camryn giggled for the first time that day.

"Ah, there is that smile I've been looking for. You like children?"

"I love them. Who doesn't?"

"You'd be surprised. One day, we'll have a few of our own, but, of course, I'd first have to bring you over."

"Children? Bring me over? What are you talking about?"

"I'd have to make you immortal before you could carry my child to term."

She gulped. "You mean make me a vampire?"

"Not necessarily. Remember I'm a hybrid so you don't necessarily have to be a vampire but our child would be part vampire at the very least."

"So anyone who mates with an immortal has to become one in order to carry immortal children."

"Just vampires actually, because of our unique physiology. I've heard of cases where shifters and warlocks have impregnated humans and a half bloods are born from those unions. But with a vampire child, so much is required to sustain that life that it could kill a human mother to carry a vampire child to term."

"I see. It sounds complicated."

"It is a process but it's not as frightening as it sounds."

"Can we slow this down for a minute?"

He sat up, not sure she meant by that statement. "Slow what down?"

"This talk of children and making me immortal. It's all too much for me to process right now."

"You don't believe our future is worth discussing or is it that you don't want children with me." Camryn had another think coming if she thought he'd allow her to get away from him again. They belonged together and if he did nothing else, he'd make sure she knew it as well.

"I didn't say that but...look. I guess we haven't had a chance to talk about this and now is probably as good a time as any to do it."

He grasped her hands. "You're not going to change your mind are you?

"Of course not, just listen okay?"

Jagger's heart thumped hard within his chest. "Okay, but before you say anything, I want you to know: *Ya lyublyu tebya*, I love you even though those words don't adequately describe how I feel about you but there it is."

"You're making it impossible for me to pull away from you aren't you?"

"Are you trying to pull away from me?"

'Would you just listen?"

He sighed. "Okay but whatever you say, won't change how I feel about you."

She squeezed his hands back "I know and I'm glad. There's a reason why I'm a little hesitant about the whole starting a family and being immortal. I've never had any luck with love. I didn't think I was capable of feeling it until you came along.

Jagger's breath caught in his throat, his heart pounded even faster. "Are you saying...?"

"That I love you, too? Yes, I do Jagger. And it scares the hell out of me."

He caressed her cheek with the back of his hand. "Why? Do you think I'd hurt you? You have to know I could never do that. You mean everything to me."

"I want to believe that—I do believe it but you have to understand where I'm coming from. I grew up in a household where my father berated and constantly put my mother down. Day in and day out she'd practically bend over backwards to please him but it was never enough for him. He would constantly cheat on her and I could see how much it hurt her but she stayed for the sake of me and my brother and because he made her feel so worthless she was afraid to leave him." She visibly shuddered as if the memory still haunted her.

Jagger's heart went out to Camryn. He could only imagine how she must have felt having witnessed that most of her life. Her father sounded like a complete idiot. His Aunt Maggie was possibly one of the kindest women he'd ever had the pleasure of knowing besides his own mother. "I mean no offense Camryn, but you father is a bully and bullies pick on people they perceive to be weaker than them to cover up their own inadequacies.

"I know that now. For a long time, I blamed myself for mom being stuck in her predicament, because if she didn't have children then maybe it would have been easier for her to leave him. It strained my relationship with her for a long time. My mom had dreams before she met my Dad but he didn't allow her to pursue them. I guess what I've come to realize recently is that I've been holding men at a distance for as long as I can remember. I didn't even realize I was doing it. This was what I meant earlier about being scared. I didn't want someone to come along and ruin the plans I have for my future. I don't want to sacrifice who I am in the name of love."

It finally made sense why Camryn had been fighting so hard and denying their attraction from the very beginning. Understandably, her childhood had scarred her in a way that made it difficult for her to give her heart to anyone. He was humbled that she was willing to try with him. "Camryn, you don't have to change who you are to be with me. I fell in love with you just the way you are. From the sound of it, your parents weren't in love because love isn't about tearing someone down. It's about building the one you love up."

"I know that now but it doesn't allay my fears. You see, from the moment I saw you, I knew you were trouble," she laughed. "You were the one who was going to challenge my ideals on love, I might not have recognized it on a conscious level at first, but subconsciously I must have always known."

"It's because we are meant to be. *Milaya moya,* you have to stop blaming yourself for what happened in the past. Your parents are not you and me. Look at your mother now. She's happy with my uncle. She has the kind of life she's always deserved. But don't allow the past to hold you back. Instead, use it as a lesson. I'm a firm believer that things happen for a reason. If your mother had not married your father, she wouldn't have had you. And if you hadn't had the experiences you did, you wouldn't be who you are. You wouldn't be the woman I love."

A tear slid down her cheek which Jagger brushed away. "I want to be with you Jagger. More than you can know but I'm still young. I want to do so many things with my life. Sure I'd like to have children, but I still have a year of grad school left and I'd like to eventually get my doctorate in my field. I'd like a career and see the world and just be selfish for a little while before I take on the responsibility of taking care of another life."

"What makes you think I'd object to any of that? Believe it or not, before I reunited with my father I had a career myself. I was an engineer and I was quite good at what I did. I, honestly, wouldn't mind pursing that field again once I get my paperwork in order to establish my residency over here." Jagger wrapped his arms around her. "It's true that love sometimes requires sacrifices and compromises on both sides but we can make this work for both of us. I want you to have the things you most desire in life and if you'd like to hold off having children or becoming an immortal, that's fine. That's the upside to being with a man like me, we have nothing but time on our hands."

"You really mean this?"

"I do. I am your biggest supporter. It is my job to make you happy. If you want to finish school in Atlanta, we can get a place down there together." He shook her gently. "Sweetheart, I'm not asking you to give up your dreams, only to allow me to be a part of them and share them with you."

Silent tears ran down her face unheeded. He assumed them to be happy ones. "I love you, Jagger. I'm only sorry it took me this long to acknowledge it."

Jagger felt like shouting his joy to the world. Finally, there were no more obstacles standing between him and his mate. He brought his lips gently down on hers, taking his time to savor the softness of her mouth beneath his. When he pulled away, she had a smile on her face.

"Mmm, that was nice."

"And there's more where that came from but we don't want to draw any unwanted attention to ourselves. Now, I have a confession."

She raised an arched brow. "Oh yeah? What?"

"Believe it or not, I was scared, too. Love is new for me as well."

Camryn snorted with apparent disbelief. "You didn't seem scared. You were relentless."

"I had to be. I wanted you very badly, and it made me more aggressive than I should have been. I know I should have taken things more slowly."

"But you were exactly what I needed. You never gave up on me, and if you hadn't persisted, I'd still be fighting. Thank you."

"For what?"

"For loving me."

"Tell me you love me again."

"I love you, Jagger."

He grinned so hard it felt like his face would split apart. He loved her so much he could almost burst. He lowered his head to kiss her but she placed her finger on her lips. "Be careful, I bite," she teased.

Jagger chuckled "I see your love for me hasn't changed your sense of humor. You see, *milaya moya*, loving me doesn't have to change who you are. This can work. I promise I'll spend the rest of my days making you happy."

He cupped her cheek and brought their mouths together. This kiss was infinitely sweeter than any they'd shared before, because this time their hearts were fully engaged.

The happiness he'd thought he'd never find was finally his. Jagger pressed Camryn down onto the picnic blanket, his cock straining against his jeans. In the back of his mind, he knew they were in a public place, but whenever Camryn was in his arms, he couldn't think properly. He cupped her breasts in his palms, his thumbs grazing her nipples till they became hardened peaks.

Camryn wrapped her arms around him with a groan, smiling widely. "Mmm, we shouldn't be doing this, but I can't help myself."

"Nor can I. Wait until we get home. There's a bed with our names on it just waiting for us."

"Mom and Dad do that a lot. They say it's because they love each other. Do you two love each other?"

Jagger looked up to see Jaxson and Adrienne standing over them. Camryn pulled away from him, a sheepish expression on her face. He refused to let go of her hand, however, unwilling to hide his feelings for Camryn with anyone.

To his surprise, it was Camryn who answered the question. "Yes, we're in love."

"Are you going to get married?" Jaxson questioned as if he were the head of the CIA.

Camryn smiled vaguely. "Not yet, but one day."

Jagger squeezed her hand reassuringly, liking the sound of that. The little boy crinkled his nose in disgust. "Well, I'm not getting married. Girls have cooties and I don't want any part of that."

Camryn burst into laughter, Jagger joined her, even though he had no idea what cooties were. It sounded funny, though.

Jaxson didn't look amused. "Adrienne has to use the bathroom."

Camryn rose, sliding her hand out of Jagger's. "I'll take her." She held the little girl by the hand and led her to the public stalls.

"Jaxson, why don't you have a seat with me until the women get back? In the meantime, you can explain to me what cooties are."

Jaxson sat down, reached into the picnic basket, and picked out a handful of grapes. "Everyone knows what cooties are. Don't they have cooties in Russia?"

"Obviously not."

"Well, maybe that won't be a bad place for me to live. My dad is going to take me and Adrienne to Italy. I'll ask him to take us to Russia, too."

"You'll like it. Tell him to take you to Gorky Park." Jagger watched as the boy steadily munched on the grapes. "You never did tell me what cooties were."

"Oh. They're girl germs," Jaxson said gravely. "No one really knows what they look like because they're invisible, but I think they look like ticks. Bobby at school told me that if you get them, your hair falls out or something. Then, you itch like crazy. I'm safe though, because I got my cootie shots and so has Adrienne."

Jagger was trying hard not to laugh because it was clear the kid actually believed in these things called cooties. "Well, I can assure you that Camryn does not have these cooties you speak of."

"I'm glad. I like her."

"I like her, too."

"Then, you should marry her. A real gentleman doesn't kiss a lady like that unless he's gonna marry her."

Jagger raised his brow. This was obviously not a little boy; he was a grown man shrunken down to child form.

"And where did you learn this?"

"I saw it on TV."

"Well, I do intend to marry Camryn. I love her very much."

Jaxson looked like he was thinking it over, then nodded. "I guess that's okay then."

And Jagger believed it. Everything would be okay from now on.

Maggie had decided to throw a party. GianMarco's partner, Oliver, had shown up, and Maggie's friend, Montana, was also there. GianMarco knew his mate was up to another one of her matchmaking schemes, and although he had to admit that Oliver seemed quite smitten with the outspoken Montana, how things went between them remained to be seen.

This was the last night the entire family would be together. Everyone would be going their separate ways in the morning. Niccolo and Sasha were headed back to L.A. sans Jagger. Romeo and his family were going back to Boston to tie up loose ends before they returned to go house-hunting in the area.

Jagger was sticking around for a few more days and then he was going back to Atlanta with Camryn. Niccolo owned a club in that area and Jagger was going to manage it while he found a house for him and Camryn. Indeed, the fact that the two of them had settled their differences had been the biggest surprise to GianMarco.

Since the night after Jagger had nearly succumbed to *la morte dolci*, his nephew and stepdaughter couldn't seem to keep their hands off each other. He was relieved Jagger was over his suffering; having experienced it himself, he wouldn't have wished it on his worst enemy. GianMarco was equally happy his stepdaughter had finally stopped fighting her attraction to his nephew. He'd always suspected she reciprocated Jagger's feelings, but hadn't thought it was his place to bring it up.

As for his mate and child, Maggie was radiant as ever, and he adored his new baby. Everything was perfect, except Dante wasn't here. GianMarco hadn't heard from his brother in days and it tore him up inside.

"Is everything okay?" His wife came from behind him, carrying Gianna.

GianMarco smiled at his two favorite girls. He was quite pleased about having a daughter and loved every hair on her little head—and didn't care who knew it. He'd always remember his little boy, but having his *bambina* helped ease the pain.

"Let me hold her. She's wants her papa, don't you, Gia?"

Maggie carefully handed the baby to him. "She's been fidgeting all day. I've fed her and just changed her diaper, but I don't know why she's so restless."

"Probably from all the stimulation around her." GianMarco kissed Gianna's curly hair and stroked her back. She gurgled. "See. I told you she needs her papa."

Maggie smiled, patting his shoulder. "Seems like you're her favorite tonight. She only wants Mommy when she's hungry."

"Well, you've heard the expressions, 'mama's boy' and 'daddy's girl.' When we have another child, we'll probably have a son, but Gia's all mine."

Maggie grinned. "Well, I guess you can change her diaper when she does number two."

GianMarco lifted his daughter in the air, contorting his face for the baby. "I don't mind. I'll cherish every second with her. They grow up so fast."

Maggie rested her head against his back. "I miss him, too," she said softly, seemingly at random.

"Yes, well, I suppose he had his reasons for not being here, but wherever he is, I hope he's happy."

"He is. He's very happy, and he's very sorry for not coming sooner."

GianMarco and Maggie whirled around to see the eldest Grimaldi brother.

"Dante!" Maggie exclaimed, throwing herself into his arms. Dante whirled her around and gave her a light kiss on the forehead.

"You look lovely as always." He placed her back on the floor. "Congratulations on your new arrival." GianMarco noticed there was a difference in the way he'd greeted Maggie. That tension no longer hung in the air between them. Something had definitely changed.

"Thank you." She beamed at him.

Dante turned to GianMarco. "I suppose this gorgeous *bambina* is my niece?"

GianMarco's first impulse was to demand where the hell his brother had been, but he was so happy to see him that he bit the question back. Besides he wanted to show off Gianna instead. "Yes, she is beautiful. Would you like to hold her?"

Cobalt eyes twinkled with longing. "May I?"

"Gia, this is your Uncle Dante."

Dante smiled at the baby. "What a day. I got to meet a new sharp-as-a-tack nephew and two precious nieces. Gia is definitely a beauty, Marco. Just like her mother." He held the cooing baby against him.

"I'm going to see to the other guests." Maggie smiled at him again before leaving the two men with the baby.

"I'm sorry for staying away, but I had to get my head together. There were—

GianMarco was so happy to see his brother he didn't care anymore about why he'd kept himself away. "Dante, you don't have to explain. I'm just glad you're finally here. You seem rested."

"I am. I stayed at Paris's house in the Hamptons; Persephone and her friend... Isis, entertained me."

GianMarco didn't miss how he'd emphasized Isis's name. He wondered if that was the reason his brother seemed different but he figured his brother would tell him when he was ready. "I'm glad your time was relaxing."

Dante shook his head. "Actually, I ended up having quite an adventure with some Hunters. Seems Gage is back. Once we deal with this *il Diavolo, il Demonio* mess, we may have to look into the situation. I've sent some agents out to investigate further."

"This sounds serious. Are the Kyriakis' all right?"

"For now, but I believe they'll have some rough times ahead, similar to what we're going through now." Dante looked down at the baby again. "She's asleep."

"Here, let me take her."

Dante transferred Gianna into her father's arms. "Congratulations, again." He took a deep breath, then looked into his brother's eyes. "I'm very happy for you and want you to know I'm sorry for how I acted. While I was away, I realized what I felt for Maggie was infatuation, pure and simple. She touched a part of me I thought had died, and I mistook it for love. I obsessed over it until it drove a wedge between us. I never want anything like that to happen between us again. I love you, Marco, and I promise, no matter what happens, we'll work out our differences before I act like a jackass again."

"I appreciate that very much. Of course you're forgiven. We're brothers. Nothing will change that."

"Thank you. That means a lot to me. I wouldn't have come between you and Maggie, you know."

"I know. I'm just glad to have you back."

"Hopefully these next few days will be quiet so I can enjoy spending that time with the family. Maybe our enemies are taking a break as well."

Speaking of *il Diavolo*, have you heard anything on that front?"

"No, and it's worrying the hell out of me. I have a bad feeling about this. We're going to have to be very careful."

GianMarco's grip tightened on his daughter. Unfortunately, he had the same foreboding.

<><><><>

"Can this all really be happening? I mean, is it really true?" Camryn wrapped her arms around Jagger's waist when he walked into her bedroom and shut the door.

271

"It's true, but I'm wondering if I should be the one asking that. I'm the one who feels like he's in the middle of a dream." Jagger's hands slid down her back and cupped her bottom in his hand, then squeezed. Instant arousal tingled between her legs.

She kissed his jaw, a feeling of happiness she'd never felt before soaring within her. "Are you sure you'll be okay moving to Atlanta with me? It will only be for a year till I finish school. Then I'll apply for a job closer to my mom so we'll be around the family."

"*Milaya moya*, I'll go wherever you lead."

"I love you, Jagger. So much, but I'm still afraid this won't last."

"Well, whenever you think such a thing, just remember this: I wanted you when you were acting like a horrible brat, so if I didn't run then, I certainly won't leave you now."

She slapped him playfully on the shoulder. "I was not a brat. I should be offended by that remark, buddy."

"Oh, you know you were a brat. There's no use denying it. Even Uncle Romeo calls you that."

She sighed in mock exasperation. "Maybe, I was a little difficult," she conceded.

"A little?" He quirked his lips.

"Okay, I was more than a bit difficult, but I'm here now, and I'm so in love with you, Nikolai Jagger Romanov-Grimaldi, that I don't know what to do with myself."

He grinned that devilish grin of his. "You might not know what to do with yourself, but I certainly do."

"Oh? And what's that?"

"I'm going to make love to you." Without preamble, he began to unbutton her shirt, placing kisses against her skin as he unfastened each button. Camryn was suddenly flooded with a burning desire as well. Her hands fumbled with his clothes. She wanted to feel his naked flesh against hers.

"You're so beautiful," he groaned when their clothes had been discarded. He lifted her into his arms and took her to bed.

Gently, Jagger covered her with his body. Love shone within the depths of his amber eyes. Camryn's heart was so filled with emotion for him, she could barely contain it all.

She opened herself for him, ready to take each inch of his delicious cock. She sighed with relief as he slid his hard shaft into her. Lifting her hips to take him deeper into her hot box, she whispered, "I love you, so much, Jagger. I don't know why I waited so long to admit it."

"I understand, my darling. Sometimes we're afraid to listen to our hearts, and you hadn't had a shining example of what love is." Jagger slowly pulled out, then slid back into her. The moment was so tender, tears swam in her eyes.

"Please kiss me." She cupped the back of his head, pulling it down until their lips touched. Their tongues met, twining and dancing in a gentle, explorative demonstration of their love for each other. Her nipples ached deliciously as they rubbed against his chest hair, the friction sending scorching balls of fire through her system.

"Camryn, *ya tak lyubyu tebya*. I love you very much."

"I love you, too." She clung to him, their bodies moving and grinding together. Her heart felt as if it would overflow with love for him. No matter what happened in the future between them, she would always have this moment. She'd trust in him and their love.

When her climax came, she screamed out her release. "Jagger! love you!"

"And I, you, *milaya moya*." When he peaked, her pussy muscles tightened around his cock, milking him of every drop he had within him. Finally, he rested his head within the crook of her neck.

Camryn ran her fingers along the along his spine. "Jagger?"

"Yes?"

"Remember when you came to my school, you said something to me in Russian? You told me you'd tell me when the time was right. Is the time right, yet?"

"Most definitely. I said, 'When I first met you, for the first time, I understood it's forever.'"

And she believed him.

Epilogue

Invite me in.

Camryn sat up in bed, startled. She'd had the strangest dream of a woman with red hair. She'd knocked on the door and Camryn had answered it. She remembered the woman asking questions and feeling compelled to answer each one. Before her eyes, the woman had turned into a monster and then, she woke up. She let out a sigh of relief to learn it had all been a dream even though it had felt so real.

She noticed her hand was really sticky. Bringing it to her line of vision, she let out a piercing scream. Her hand was covered in blood!

Jagger wasn't in bed with her. Her heart plummeted in terror as she looked around the room to see blood not only saturating the bed, but spread on the carpets and smeared on the walls. Was this some kind of crazy nightmare? Was she still dreaming?

She slid out of bed and grabbed her robe, miraculously blood free, from the foot of the bed. The sun was just beginning to rise.

"Jagger!" she screamed his name as she sprinted through the halls and banged on every bedroom door in the house, shouting frantically. Dante was the first one out of the bed. His eyes widened when he saw the blood on her hands.

"What's happened?"

"I don't know. Jagger wasn't in bed when I woke and the room is covered in blood. I think it's his." Tears ran down her face. This couldn't be happening.

Niccolo whirled her around to face him, face more pale than usual. "What's happened to my son?"

"I don't know," she whispered.

Sasha raced to the bedroom where Camryn and Jagger had spent the night. "My baby!"

Another scream filled the house, followed quickly by another. The men took off to investigate, Camryn on their tails. She looked into a bedroom to see Romeo and Christine tearing the room apart. They looked as panicked as the others.

"Jaxson isn't here." Romeo said as he ran out of the room. "I'm going to check Adrienne's room."

Camryn had a sinking feeling. Jagger was missing, and now Jaxson and possibly Adrienne. She gasped. Mom!

Camryn ran to the nursery to see her mother lying in a heap, sobbing in hysterics. GianMarco had lost all color and looked to be in shock.

"Not again. Not again," he muttered over and over again.

"Mom?" Camryn was too scared to check the crib. She slowly moved toward it and sucked in a breath when she looked in. Only a crumpled bloody blanket lay there.

She passed out.

Dante tore through the house searching for his nieces and nephews even though he had an awful feeling they were no longer there. He ran outside to seek out any clues he could find. There had to be something.

This was his fault. He shouldn't have stayed away from his family for so long. He should have been diligently working to track Adonis down. Instead, he'd allowed this to happen. Because of him, the children were missing and possibly dead. Hadn't his brothers suffered enough without this? How had the rogues gotten into the house? Though the rooms were soundproofed, surely someone would have heard the children being taken? And judging by the quantity of blood in Jagger's room, why hadn't Camryn woken up?

This travesty had Adonis written all over it. Dante knew if the children didn't make it, his brothers would never recover.

This was the final straw. They'd fucked with the Grimaldis for the last time.

It was time the rogues felt the full weight of his wrath.

About the Author

NYT and USA Today Bestselling Author Eve Vaughn has always enjoyed creating characters and stories from an early age. As a child she was always getting into mischief, so when she lost her television privileges (which was often), writing was her outlet. Her stories have gotten quite a bit spicier since then! When she's not writing or spending time with her family, Eve is reading, baking, traveling or kicking butt in 80's trivia. She loves hearing from her readers. She can be contacted through her website at: www.evevaughn.com.

Books by Eve Vaughn:

Whatever He Wants

Dirty

Run

The Auction

Jilted

The Kyriakis Curse:
Book One of the Kyriakis Series

GianMarco:
Book One of the Blood Brothers Series

Niccolo:
Book Two of the Blood Brothers Series

Romeo:
Book Three of the Blood Brothers Series

Made in the USA
Monee, IL
07 November 2021